"GET YOUR CLOTHES OFF, MISTER!"

Fargo stared at her. "What's the name, miss?"
What different will that make?"

"I like to know a woman's name when I get
into bed with her."

"Well, I don't give a damn what your name is."
She studied him. "You look like you could be
a big man, but I don't see any excitement here."

She had a damned shapely body, fine shoulders,
firm breasts, a soft rounded belly, full hips. Skye
could feel desire stirring but he wasn't going
to let her have it all her own way.

"You've got a good body, honey, but I'll tell
you, honestly, something about being forced puts
me off."

"Well, you better put it up, mister, or we may
have to put you down."

Skye grinned. If that was the game she was
playing he was going to teach her some new
rules that would have her begging for more . . .

Exciting Westerns by Jon Sharpe from SIGNET

(0451)

- [ ] **THE TRAILSMAN #1: SEVEN WAGONS WEST**
  (110528—$2.25)
- [ ] **THE TRAILSMAN #2: THE HANGING TRAIL** (110536—$2.25)
- [ ] **THE TRAILSMAN #3: MOUNTAIN MAN KILL** (121007—$2.50)*
- [ ] **THE TRAILSMAN #4: THE SUNDOWN SEARCHERS**
  (122003—$2.50)*
- [ ] **THE TRAILSMAN #5: THE RIVER RAIDERS** (111990—$2.25)
- [ ] **THE TRAILSMAN #6: DAKOTA WILD** (119886—$2.50)*
- [ ] **THE TRAILSMAN #7: WOLF COUNTRY** (099052—$2.25)*
- [ ] **THE TRAILSMAN #8: SIX-GUN DRIVE** (121724—$2.50)*
- [ ] **THE TRAILSMAN #9: DEAD MAN'S SADDLE** (112806—$2.25)*
- [ ] **THE TRAILSMAN #10: SLAVE HUNTER** (114655—$2.25)
- [ ] **THE TRAILSMAN #11: MONTANA MAIDEN** (116321—$2.25)
- [ ] **THE TRAILSMAN #12: CONDOR PASS** (118375—$2.50)*
- [ ] **THE TRAILSMAN #13: BLOOD CHASE** (119274—$2.50)*
- [ ] **THE TRAILSMAN #14: ARROWHEAD TERRITORY**
  (120809—$2.50)*
- [ ] **THE TRAILSMAN #15: THE STALKING HORSE**
  (121430—$2.50)*
- [ ] **THE TRAILSMAN #16: SAVAGE SHOWDOWN**
  (122496—$2.50)*
- [ ] **THE TRAILSMAN #17: RIDE THE WILD SHADOW**
  (122801—$2.50)*
- [ ] **THE TRAILSMAN #18: CRY THE CHEYENNE**
  (123433—$2.50)*

*Prices slightly higher in Canada

THE TRAILSMAN 19

SPOON RIVER STUD

by
Jon Sharpe

A SIGNET BOOK
NEW AMERICAN LIBRARY
TIMES MIRROR

NAL BOOKS ARE AVAILABLE AT QUANTITY DISCOUNTS
WHEN USED TO PROMOTE PRODUCTS OR SERVICES.
FOR INFORMATION PLEASE WRITE TO PREMIUM MARKETING DIVISION,
THE NEW AMERICAN LIBRARY, INC., 1633 BROADWAY,
NEW YORK, NEW YORK 10019.

SIGNET TRADEMARK REG. U.S. PAT. OFF. AND FOREIGN COUNTRIES
REGISTERED TRADEMARK—MARCA REGISTRADA
HECHO EN CHICAGO, U.S.A.

SIGNET, SIGNET CLASSICS, MENTOR, PLUME, MERIDIAN and NAL BOOKS are published by The New American Library, Inc., 1633 Broadway, New York, New York 10019

First Printing, July, 1983

1 2 3 4 5 6 7 8 9

PRINTED IN THE UNITED STATES OF AMERICA

The Trailsman

Beginnings . . . they bend the tree and they mark the man. Skye Fargo was born when he was eighteen. Terror was his midwife, vengeance his first cry. Killing spawned Skye Fargo, ruthless, cold-blooded murder. Out of the acrid smoke of gunpowder still hanging in the air, he rose, cried out a promise never forgotten.

The Trailsman, they began to call him, all across the West: searcher, scout, hunter, the man who could see where others only looked, his skills for hire but not his soul, the man who lived each day to the fullest, yet trailed each tomorrow. Skye Fargo, the Trailsman, the seeker who could take the wildness of a land and the wanting of a woman and make them his own.

*The early 1860s—Spoon River,
a town in the Dakota Territory,
where strong men live by
the gun or die by it.*

1

Three days of hard riding had left Fargo almost too tired to sleep. His nerves were frayed from forcing himself too far, too long. He needed a good sound sleep, the kind that gives a man back body and mind.

For the last hour the sun pounded on him like a hammer, and now at last he was hit with sudden drowsiness. The lake-blue eyes in the bronzed square face slid almost shut. He had stopped hours ago at the saloon in Spoon River and the one shot of whiskey, lousy at that, hadn't helped keep him alert. He stared at a great spreading oak with a thick trunk stuck in the earth; its cool shade beckoned him. He mopped his neck; the intense heat even hit his loins, and his body seethed. He cursed, nudged the sweating Ovaro to the oak, and when he reached the shade, his big, lean, muscled body slipped off the horse. He crawled on the cool carpeted grass to the trunk, leaned against it, shut his eyes and was asleep in moments.

Only a minute it seemed could have passed when he felt himself snap awake. He wasn't alone, and he felt a sudden kick against his boot.

"Hey!" A woman's voice, throaty, sexy. Slowly his eyes focused on her. The kick came again.

"Looks like a live one," a voice said.

His eyes now fully open, he found himself

staring at three women. The three women each held a gun. No damn little dance-hall pistols, but real six-guns.

He shut his eyes, then opened them, expecting the women would be gone. But they weren't, and they weren't smiling either. The blond woman nearest, the one who kicked his boot, had cobalt-blue eyes, and the gun she held was rock-steady. There were two good-looking women behind her, and they didn't look friendly either. But they did look familiar.

"What's the name, cowboy?" the blonde asked.

He started to get up, cursing inwardly. He'd paid the price for running himself into a near exhaustion.

"Don't move till I tell you," she said sharply.

He stared into her blue eyes, and they looked deadly serious. She had a saucy, long-lipped mouth, a pert pretty face, and wore, as did the others, tailored riding breeches, a checked shirt, and fine leather boots.

"The name is Skye Fargo. And don't get nervous. You've got three guns."

She nodded. "And you won't look good with three holes. Get his gun, Maude."

Maude, a redhead with white skin and a fine expanse of chest, bent toward his right holster. He was ready to make a lightning grab, use the redhead for cover, pull his gun, but the blonde, watching like a hawk, did some thought-reading.

"No tricks, Fargo, or you're already gone."

He smiled slowly. She was fast, a gun-smart filly, but he didn't like finding himself looking into her gun like this. Still, he was eaten up with curiosity: what in hell did they want with him? Money, guns, the horse? They didn't seem to need such things; they looked well-fed, well-cared-for, respectable—even prosperous.

Maude, the redhead, flung his gun into a cluster of bushes, and then she and the other woman, a black-eyed brunette, holstered their guns.

Now they looked him over, every inch of his body, it seemed, the way you'd look at a horse before you bought it. Would they look at his teeth, too? he wondered.

He, in turn, stared back, but that didn't faze them one bit. Suddenly it hit him why they looked familiar. He'd seen the redhead and the brunette in the general store that very morning in Spoon River. Just a glimpse, for he'd been in a hurry, but he remembered they were both well-shaped and looked like respectable married women.

The blonde moved her gun slightly and it was now pointed, he was aware, directly toward his heart.

"What's the gun for, missy?"

"To keep you well-behaved. And the name is Abigail."

"I'll behave," he said.

Again the silence and the looking.

"Are you going to buy me?" he asked suddenly.

Abigail's eyebrows rose sharply. "Why'd you say that?"

"You're looking at me like I'm a slab of meat."

Abigail grimaced. "In a way, Fargo, you are." She turned to the brunette. "Give him some whiskey, Julia."

Julia walked to the horses grazing under a nearby maple, took a bottle and a tin cup from the saddlebag. When she gave him the cup, it was almost half-full.

"Not a bad idea." He gulped down some of it.

"Drink it all," Abigail commanded.

"Why not?" He grinned. It was all friendly enough, and it seemed she wasn't going to shoot him, after all.

"Give him another."

He looked at Julia while she poured again: glowing black eyes in a face that was pretty but a bit hard. She studied him without smiling, then started toward the horses, joined by Maude.

He sipped the drink.

"Drink it all," Abigail said.

He gazed at her. "So that's your evil game?"

She frowned. "What?"

"You trailed me, woke me, stole my gun. All this to get me drunk."

She smiled. "No, Fargo. I want you to have a few drinks to cushion the shock."

He scowled. "Shock? What shock?" There was no way of figuring this woman. Was she going to shoot him for kicks?

Her smile stayed fixed, as though it were painted on. "Fargo, you're a lucky man. We're going to give you the privilege of having a tumble with two lovely women." She jerked her thumb at Maude and Julia.

Fargo stared. She might be smiling, but she seemed dead serious.

"Give me that again?"

Her eyes never wavered. "I think you heard me."

He spoke slowly. "You mean, you did all this— threatened to shoot, stole my gun, pumped me with liquor—to force me to tumble those two ladies?"

"Yes, I suppose I did." Her tone was level.

He stroked his chin. She had an upturned nose, a saucy mouth, and under those tailored riding pants, a damned shapely body. If he had to tumble someone, she'd have been his first choice.

"Why didn't you just ask politely?" he said.

She leaned forward, as if she didn't get it. "What?"

"If you wanted me to bed the ladies, why didn't you just ask me?" He glanced about, saw only Julia with the horses. Where was the other?

Abigail squinted. "Are you trying to trick me, Fargo? Because if you are, you won't get away with it."

He shook his head. "I'm more than happy to oblige the ladies." He grinned. "I was never in a better mood for it."

Her face was grim as she studied him. "You mean it, don't you? You don't mind playing stud?"

That hit him wrong, somehow. "Playing stud," sounded as though it were something low-down. He didn't like it, but pushed the thought out of his mind. Instead he remembered that he hadn't had a woman for a week, that he'd been horny as a goat. And that the booze was already buzzing in his veins.

"The truth is, Abigail, I feel like a sex-starved stallion."

Her mouth twisted and her smile was not nice. "Men always brag about their sex powers, don't they, Fargo?" She pointed behind him. About two hundred feet away there was a hedge of bushes about ten feet high, a neat hideaway, most likely. "Go there. You'll find Maude waiting. See if she likes stallions."

Fargo stared at her. She was one damned peculiar filly. "Tell me, these ladies, who could get any man just by whistling—just why are they doing this?"

Her face hardened. She had a look like steel

13

under silk. "That, Fargo, is none of your damn business. And you're not to ask them. Just do it."

He nodded. He liked the way she fenced his questions, the mocking smile, the saucy mouth, the round thrust of her breasts, the way she handled herself. "Are you sure you don't want to jump in this game? I'm ready when you are."

The direct blue eyes drilled right through him. "That will be the day, cowboy." Her hard tone jolted him, and he wondered if she were angry at the sex game the other ladies were playing. Did she work for them, perhaps? he wondered. Did she have a yen to get into the act, but was fighting it? He threw that idea away as something he'd like to believe. He glanced at the hedges and pictured the redhead already there, ready for play. His body responded. He stood and the bulge in his britches couldn't help catch her eye. But she maintained her nice control.

"Just a minute, Fargo. This is a one-shot thing. After it's over, you just keep riding, you understand? It will be finished for all time."

His smile was cool; nothing, he thought, is ever finished for all time.

He started toward the hedges, his loins loaded for action. But there was still a burr at the back of his brain. He glanced over at Abigail; she still held the gun, her face unsmiling. Julia, watching them from near the horses, also kept her hand near her holster. As he walked, he felt strongly aware of their hard eyes, observing him, then came the sting of anger. This was force, and he didn't like it. He had tried a checkmate, turning what they wanted at the point of a gun into an act of fun. He tried to make it a game, but they kept pushing, and he didn't like to be pushed—in anything.

The anger squelched desire, and by the time he went behind the hedges, the commotion in his britches had subsided.

Still, the sight of Maude jolted him. She had spread a bedroll on the grass and was sitting upon it. She wore a silky chemise that revealed most of her breasts, nicely sized, her thighs and legs milk-white and shapely. Her red hair was knotted behind her head; she had blue-green eyes and full sensuous lips. A sexy piece, all right. But still he felt the anger.

She glanced up at him. "Hurry, cowboy. Get your clothes off. You've got a hard day ahead."

He cocked his head. "You're not a bad-looking woman."

She scowled. "I'm not interested in your opinion. Don't waste time."

His jaw clamped. She was pretty bitchy. Would that put an added edge to the action? He bent to his boots. "Try to be womanly. I'd like that better."

Her lips twisted almost in a sneer. "I don't give a damn what you like. We're not having an affair."

"What are we having?"

"Just a fast roll. Hurry and get this over with."

He scowled. She had about as much charm as a warthog.

He pulled his shirt off. "You've got lousy manners, Maude."

She stared back, as though almost in shock. "Who the hell do you think you are, cowboy? We grab you off the trail, offer you a shot any man would give his right arm for, and you talk about manners. Just do what you're supposed to and get the hell off."

Fargo grimaced. She was so nasty he felt the

kind of sex coming on that had to have a core of anger. The thought hit him that the only way to get any pleasure out of this bitch was to lash her tail and then screw her silly. He pulled off his jeans and then his underpants.

She studied him with interest. "You look like you're pretty big, but I don't see any excitement here."

His smile was cold. "To tell the truth, Maude, I don't see anything exciting here either."

She flushed and her eyes narrowed. Then she slipped off her chemise. She had a damned shapely body, fine shoulders, firm breasts with brown nipples, a soft rounded belly, full hips, and red fuzz over her triangle. He felt a quick shot of desire, but made no effort to encourage it. He'd rather not cooperate with this one.

"You've got a good body, Maude, but I'll tell you, honestly, something about being forced puts me off."

She scowled. "Well, mister, you better put it up or we may have to put you down."

He grinned. Yes, the only way—to bang hell out of the bitch. Make her work for it and then pay her off.

"I wonder, lady, if it's possible to rape a man? There should be a way of starting it." He stepped in front of her.

Her blue-green eyes glittered with anger, but she stared at his maleness, which now hung heavy with the promise of power. Her breathing quickened, and as if aware there could be a lot of excitement here if she played his game, she flashed him a sullen look, then dropped between his knees. She took hold of him, pressed her face against him; then, stirred by awakening passion, she kissed and caressed him. Then, in a sudden surge of excitement, her mouth began a frenzy of movement. It went on and on, and he had to give in to the sheer pleasure in watching. She suddenly stopped, looked at his pulsating potency, and then said. "You see how easy it is to rape a man?"

She slid back on the bedroll, her legs spread apart, and looked up at him. He felt hard now with lust and there was just one way to go. He'd shaft her until she hollered uncle.

He crawled nimbly over her body, grabbed her breasts, touched the already erect nipples, but he didn't waste a moment with tenderness. He slipped quickly into the red fuzz mat to the inner warmth, thrusting firmly so that he went in all the way, and then heard the sharp intake of her breath. He was very large and she was nice and tight against his flesh; she felt it too, for she began to squirm and groan. He began slowly, then went fast, and because she'd been so bitchy, he thrust his body against her hard, grabbing her silky butt with his strong hands, then pounding, making it a punishing kind of sex. This was how to do it, all right. The lady wanted sex—well, he'd give it to her in spades. He could hear her sharp gasps, her little squeals, her groans, and he knew it all sounded wild; and it was hard to tell whether it was pain or pleasure she felt, but he couldn't stop now. He felt her fingers gripping his back, the nails cutting into his flesh, and the pulling infuriated him. He thrust more violently, felt the great surge and anguish as he went into climax. As for her, poor thing, she lay squirming from side to side, hissing through her clenched teeth, as if he had violated her with an ax in addition to his mighty maleness.

He smiled grimly. She had wanted force—well,

he'd given it. And honestly, for him it had been a great ride.

He looked down at her red, flushed face, expecting to see anger, fury, expecting a tigress to rip back at him. But her damned face was now even radiant, her eyes looked starry. Son of a bitch, he thought, when it comes to sex, you can't match a woman. You think you're beating them silly, and instead you're booting them into paradise!

Fargo was alone behind the hedges when he caught the strong smell of frying rabbit. He'd been thinking about Maude, who in spite of herself, had gone hellbent for heaven. Then he heard Abigail call out.

"Fargo! We've got some food. Come out."

He realized he had been sensing the pangs of hunger. He slipped into his pants and grinned; they wanted to keep the stud well-fed so he could do the job properly.

Abigail's blue eyes glittered at him. She's trying to read me, to see if I liked it or hated it, he thought. She's a dilly.

Obviously not a trusting woman, she still held the gun and used it to point toward the meat now crispy brown in the fry pan. A pot of coffee simmered over the fire.

"To keep up your strength." Her mouth twisted with amusement.

"Yes, sex does leave a man hungry." He sat opposite her, dug into the meat, and chewed it with enjoyment. She watched, eyes alert, her face a mask. About a hundred feet away, Maude and Julia were in a huddle near the horses.

He said nothing until he cleaned off his plate and started on the coffee.

"What's your tie-in with these ladies?"

"Tie-in?" She smiled. "I'm the top gun, that's the tie-in."

He grinned. The chippie had a helluva confidence, and it wouldn't surprise him one damned bit if she could sharpshoot with the best. "I'm sure you can shoot the hair off a gnat's nose. But I mean something else."

"What do you mean, Fargo?"

"The women here want a party. Why are you left out?"

She smiled insolently. "I've told you. I don't want a party."

He stayed with it. "But don't you feel left out?"

She stared coldly, didn't even answer.

He shook his head. "It's one big puzzle."

Her lip curled. "Don't bother your head about it, Fargo."

He sensed a slithering movement ten feet from her. "Who shot the rabbit?" he asked casually.

Her saucy mouth smiled. "I did."

"Good." His tone was still casual. "You'll have to shoot a reptile ten feet to your left."

The blue eyes stared hard at him. "A trick, Fargo?" But she'd been alerted, and when the slithering started again, she fired. The snake, brown and thick, at least five feet long, jumped up, curling in agony, then went still. Its black small eyes still looked deadly.

"Son of a bitch," she said. Then her face went soft. "Thanks, Fargo."

He lifted his coffeecup. "You're not a bad shot," he said.

She looked at the snake with distaste, turned to signal the startled women with the horses that all was well.

"Why do you want me to keep riding afterward?" he asked.

"It will be a lot healthier." Her pert face went grim.

"I'm not sure of that."

"What do you mean?"

"Facing two sex-hungry women can be more dangerous than facing anything else."

She shrugged and her gaze traveled over his body, lingering at the bulge in his britches. "Somehow, Fargo, I think you won't go down in defeat." She pointed her gun. "Now that you're rejuvenated, you can go back."

Again Fargo felt the sting of anger. In spite of joking and the rambunctious kick he got from his romp with Maude, he didn't like force. He liked to pick his target and he didn't like to be pushed to perform like a stud. He glanced at the plate as a weapon for diversion.

"Fargo!" The soft female voice had an edge of iron. "No tricks." Then her tone softened. "Just do your job and you'll get out of this with your skin whole." She watched him stand, his eyes glittering. "After all, laying with a beautiful woman is a lot better than laying in a cold, lonely grave."

He scowled. "If you don't choose the woman, it's not that much better."

He still smoldered as he walked back behind the hedges. Julia sat there in a pink chemise, with a bottle in her hand, and she looked a touch soused.

She was almost plump, with heavy breasts, nipples that stuck against the silk of the chemise. She had a well-shaped nose, a full lower lip, liquid black eyes, and sleek black hair that framed her milk-white skin. Her pretty face was frowning,

20

as if she, too, didn't really go for this odd situation. But something about her still looked interested. She didn't come at him like Maude, ready to slug. Even looked a touch embarrassed. She poured a drink, gulped it. He grinned. Nothing whorish here—it seemed it was a strange experience for her; it might even be the first time she had tried it with a stranger passing through.

"I suppose we ought to hurry and get it over with." She lifted her chemise. She had a soft, rounded tummy and a luxurious patch of black hair between her thighs.

He smiled. "Hurry won't do a thing for pleasure, Julia."

She grimaced. "I don't think I'm supposed to be doing this for pleasure."

"What are you doing it for?" he asked quickly. She was half-soused and might spring the real reason.

Her lids fluttered over her black eyes. She had a touch of modesty, and he felt good about her for that.

"I can't tell you. Let's just go ahead. There isn't much time."

He slipped off his clothes, and as she waited, she took another generous swallow.

When he peeled off his britches, her eyes stared at him, fascinated. She had ticked off the right feelings and he knew how aroused he looked to her. He moved quickly, put his arms around her, and at the very touch of his flesh against hers, her breathing instantly quickened. She sat waiting, a pliant woman. He kissed her full lips, kept at it, and soon her mouth responded. He took her hand, put it over his throbbing rod of excitement. She pulled away as though it were a hot iron. He brought her back, and within moments she held him so hard it almost hurt; her mouth started to work against his lips.

His finger went down to her triangle and he stroked it, at first gently, then pushing into the lush, liquid warmth. She was hit by a great surge of passion and her mouth dropped open.

He let the fires build, then dropped to her breasts, stroked the nipple of each with his tongue. He caressed her curved voluptuous body, feeling the contours of her buttocks. And along with all the rest, he kept moving his finger back and forth. She went limp with desire and they went down together to the bedroll, her face moving instantly close to his organ of excitement. She went for it with a natural appetite and made guttural sounds of pleasure. He felt a series of erotic waves, then slipped over her body and eased his bigness into her, he started slowly, but he quickly reached a pitch of passion and began to pummel her, moving in and out, his hands holding onto her buttocks. Her curved smooth body gave him intense pleasure, and he kept thrusting, coming almost out, driving in, feeling her body rising in rhythm. It went on and on, and he glanced down to see her suffering agonies of joy. He drove harder, then his body tightened and he mobilized and exploded; she, too, went off, groaning like an animal in pain, flinging herself against his body, holding him with a deadly grip.

He stayed within her a short while; then, as he started to rise, her hands went out, as if to hold him longer.

He looked down at her white body with its plump breasts and tangle of dark hair at her pubis; her thighs were still trembling. She raised her eyes and there was a strange expression in their blackness.

"Fargo, you bastard. I should never have done this." She looked away, her face tense. "It won't ever be this good again for me."

Much later, Fargo watched Maude and Julia mount their horses and start off in a canter toward Spoon River. Meanwhile, Abigail swung over her gelding before him, still holding her gun, but her voice was friendly.

"Be smart, Fargo. Don't follow. Just keep on riding." Her blue eyes glinted strangely. "I think you gave much more than was expected. I'm sure the ladies were grateful. Good-bye and good luck."

She spurred the horse, which shot into a full gallop. She rode smooth as cream. He watched until she disappeared around a turn of trees, and then he smiled. She was a ding-a-ling and easily the sweetest honey of them all. The one who got away. But you don't get everything you want in this world. Well, he'd go on now to Devil's Crossing, the place where he had been heading, trying to run down a lead on the low-down skunk he'd been tracking for vengeance.

He scoured the bushes for his gun, and when he found it, he gave it a thorough cleaning. The Ovaro had been grazing in a rich patch of grass. Fargo brushed and coddled him, then swung into the saddle. For one long moment he was tempted to turn east to Spoon River. Three beautiful women. It was intriguing. What made them do it? What was it all about? There were answers in Spoon River. But maybe it was better not to find them. After all, he didn't exactly hate what had happened, did he?

He shrugged it off and turned the Ovaro west.

After a few hours' riding, he camped for the

night near a small stream. He watched a quarter moon slowly climb while his beans and beef jerky heated over a fire in a dug pit. It never paid to advertise your whereabouts in this wild country, he thought, where man and animal, even man and man, preyed on each other. Still, the smell of frying beef drifted out and a coyote began to skulk around the edge of the camp. As he bit into the beef, he noted the Ovaro was chafing nervously. It's a hungry bitch of a coyote, he thought, and flung a couple of stones. The animal ducked and crept around until Fargo, aware it would be a bad night, regretfully pulled his gun and, at the next sight of the glittering eyes, drilled a hole between them. After that, the pinto went quiet, as did the night—that is, everything but his dreams, which, in spite of his recent sackful of sex, still continued erotic.

Curiously he dreamed not of the women he had lain with, but of the one he did not, the irresistible Abigail. In his dream she tossed her gun away and told him that, since he was such a pistol, she, too, wouldn't mind a tumble. He started to her, but she slipped away, behind the hedges, and hard as he looked, he couldn't find her. She had teased him, he thought, which left him furious. He was thrashing through the hedges when he was awakened by the shrill cry of a hawk that had just speared its prey. It was now daylight.

As he sipped hot coffee from his tin cup and meditated on the dream, he knew that the one woman who had truly reached him was the one he never caught. He thought about it as the pinto cantered west, and he realized that his urge to go back to Spoon River came not only from a desire to solve the mystery of the women, but because

24

Abigail was an unfinished story. Not only was she as pert a piece as he'd ever seen, but she was smart, sharp, and gun-wise.

He sighed, tried to put her out of his mind and focus instead on the world around him. Now the sun hit the earth gently and the grass and flowers gleamed with rich midsummer color. Ahead of him, the golden rays turned the great range of mountains to the west into a massive bronze monument of stone.

The pinto moved at a leisurely pace, its great muscles rippling smoothly, and Fargo felt a sudden lightness, a stab of pleasure; it was a feeling that came often when he drifted out of the towns of men, a man alone on the trail, depending on his own skills to survive in a world of danger.

It was in this mood, looking at a stone shaped like a pike pointing toward heaven, when a shiver went through him. It was so slight a feeling that if he had not been trained long ago to stay alert to such signals from deep in his primitive alarm system, he would have bypassed it. But he didn't, he never did. Yet there was nothing about that even hinted danger. He turned the pinto toward a mass of rock, piled on each other, climbing at least five hundred feet. He felt his body go tense in the saddle. Still he could see nothing. At the rocks he started to climb, and a hundred feet up, he worked more carefully, for movement was the great betrayer. When he got to a commanding view of the terrain, he stepped into a crevice and studied the land below.

Three riders were racing down a slope, hellbent on something or someone.

The men looked tough, with short-brimmed black hats, leather vests, and each holstered two guns. Gunslingers on a hunt. But who was the quarry? They came to a halt and studied tracks. Whose? His tracks were the freshest. Could he be the quarry? But why? In Spoon River, he had stopped just for supplies, and a fast lousy whiskey at Denny's Saloon. No trouble there. Of course, they could be blood kin to men he had killed in the past, deeds regrettable but unavoidable when a man was entitled to seek revenge. Not likely, in this case. These men sure looked ready for a killing; he was able to smell that sort of thing.

He watched and remembered that near a certain rock cluster he had turned sharp off the trail to follow the tracks of a possum, which after a half-mile crisscrossed the track of coyotes, also interested in lunch. At that point, he swung back to the trail.

The riders shortly reached the rock cluster, stopped, followed his tracks to swing back on the trail. His jaw hardened. They were after him, and he didn't have much time.

A quarter-mile west, scattered boulders looked like a good place to take cover. He came down the crags with care, hit the ground, then moved at high speed, putting the pinto into a hard run. They were three, and he was one, to equalize this, he needed surprise.

When he reached the boulders, he tethered the pinto out of sight, pulled his Colt, and settled down to wait.

Minutes dragged. His boot scuffed the earth and a gray mouse with bold, beady eyes stuck his nose out of a hole, curious to know who was invading his domain. The mouse streaked back. Fargo smiled. Everyone has his own territory, he thought.

He waited and felt the heat of a hard sun hit

the hand that cradled his gun. He had a good position behind the boulder, and visibility of the trail for two hundred feet.

Then he heard the drumbeat of hooves against the earth and saw the riders coming in a file at a fast canter.

He put a bullet in front of the first horse, a sorrel, which snorted, pawed at the sky as the rider pulled hard on the bridle.

"Hold it right there," Fargo called. The rider of the sorrel had a narrow cruel face with mean eyes, a vicious scar on his jaw. The riders behind also pulled up, their horses twisting and snorting at the hard bridling. The second rider had wild eyes and a red bandanna on his neck; the third rider looked very young, as if he didn't quite belong with such hard characters.

Fargo came out, gun in hand. "No wrong moves," he advised.

Scarface stared, his dark eyes taking in Fargo's face and body.

Fargo smiled, as though friendly, and said, "Where you pilgrims heading?"

Scarface scowled. Not a man who justified his moves; gunslingers usually didn't, Fargo thought.

"What the hell difference does it make to you? We're just riding. It's a free country."

"Makes a difference," Fargo said. "Where you from?"

Scarface scowled. "Why'd you shoot at my horse?"

Fargo nodded pleasantly. "I thought it might be nice to have a little talk. Where you from?"

Scarface looked grim. "Spoon River." He paused. "You're pretty nervy, cowpoke. You're one gun. We're three guns. You're not talking smart for a man who likes living."

Fargo grinned. "Just keep in mind that if any-body here stops living, it won't be me."

The dark eyes in the narrow face slitted. He took slow, careful measure of Fargo.

"Listen, mister," he said, a crafty look in his eye. "We're on our way to Devil's Crossing. We got no quarrel with you. Don't even know who you are. We want no trouble."

Fargo studied him. The second rider, the one with the wild blue eyes, for the last minute had been inching his hand to his holster. Fargo seemed not to look at him.

"No, maybe you don't know me. My name is Fargo. And I don't want any trouble."

Just as he might have expected, his name trig-gered the nerves of the man with the wild eyes who itched to be a hero; he went for his gun. Fargo drilled a bullet into his forehead that blew the back of his skull off. He dropped from his horse in slow motion, crashing to the ground, where he fell facedown, his blood bubbling in the wound.

The horses stamped, but the riders froze, star-ing at their fallen comrade. Although Scarface was jolted, he made a quick recovery. "You had no call to do that, Fargo." His voice was deadly, guttural, his eyes small black pits.

"Your pal went for his gun," Fargo said easily. "Didn't care for my name, I reckon."

There was a heavy moment of silence. "All we wanted, mister, was to get going," said Scarface. "We didn't want no trouble like that."

Fargo nodded, grimly. "Then tell me, why were you tracking me?"

Scarface's eyes widened, but he handled it coolly. He shook his head, his face all innocence. "I swear you got it dead wrong. We were looking at tracks, yes, but we were tracking food. We followed a possum. No, you're wrong, Fargo, we had no quarrel with you. All we want now is to be on our way to Devil's Crossing and take this man home."

Fargo nodded, scratched his cheek, apparently convinced. He slipped his gun into the holster. "I guess I made a mistake. I'm sorry about your friend. He moved too quick. Go ahead, then."

And then just as Fargo sensed, Scarface made his move. It was fast. His gun was out of the holster, but before that, Fargo had hit him twice in the chest. He catapulted back, fell off his horse, squirming, his heart spouting blood like a faucet. The third rider used the shooting time to drive his horse directly at Fargo, bringing up his gun. Fargo spun to his right as he fired, hitting the younger man's chest. He fell forward, got caught in the stirrup, and was dragged past Fargo. It took a fast leap to catch the bridle and bring the horse to a stop. He eased the man from the saddle to the ground, loosened his bloody shirt. He was indeed young, with pink cheeks, a soft mouth, and brown eyes clouded with pain.

Fargo felt a stab of pity, a kid cut off before he had lived because he mixed with the wrong men. "How'd you get tied up with these killers?" he asked, cradling the young man's head.

The brown eyes looked up, pain in them. "My brother."

His breathing came hard. He'd be gone in a minute. The blood leaked from his chest. The look of death was in his eyes.

"Who sent you after me, boy?"

The eyes stared dully. He was slipping away. His eyes were going empty. He was taking the secret with him.

Fargo's teeth clenched. He leaned to the man's ear. "Who?" he tried again.

The eyes were open, empty; he was going fast. Then suddenly the lips moved, whispered, and Fargo heard one word: "Terry."

Then the eyes went glassy and the youth was dead.

Fargo dug three graves, and after he had filled in the earth, he leaned on his shovel and deliberated.

Terry? Who the hell was Terry? Why did he send three executioners after him? Why? He had never tangled with anyone called Terry. Still, this man must have had a hard grievance to send three such killers.

The answer had to lie back in Spoon River. And strangely, he had spent only thirty minutes there, buying supplies at the general store and having one or two lousy whiskies at Denny's Saloon.

He packed the shovel in his saddlebag, threw a leg over the pinto. Then he felt a quick sense of satisfaction. He had never liked leaving unsolved the riddle of his forced encounter with the women. It had preyed in the back of his mind all the time he was on the trail. Now he had a second riddle to solve: why a man called Terry had wanted him dead.

A grim smile settled on his face as he turned the Ovaro around and headed back toward Spoon River.

2

The sun glowed on the horizon, and he had come only a mile from Spoon River when he saw the buggy spinning smartly along, a shiny, elegant black buggy pulled by two prancing grays. And in it a woman just as elegant sat next to the bulky driver; she wore a silky, flashy red dress, cut low to show a hefty white bosom. Her cheeks were reddened, her eyes darkened, and her mouth shaped like a Cupid's bow. His bold stare at first seemed to bother her, but as she studied him, her face softened to a smile.

Spoon River, he thought, sure has some knock-out women.

The town, when he reached it, was like a lot of others: still frontier-rough, trying to civilize, but not having too much luck with its mix of drifters, gunmen, desperadoes among the solid citizens.

He stopped at Denny's Saloon, tied the pinto to the post, next to a powerful gelding. He pushed through the swinging doors into the spacious saloon; four men stood at the bar and five sat at a table nearby, playing cards. They all turned; you always look at a stranger, especially one with a gun. The players went back to the game; the men at the bar, wranglers, though curious, knew how to mind their business.

Denny came up, a lean, hollow-cheeked man

with sad wise eyes, the sort that's seen most things and learned to live with them. Two days ago, taking him for a stranger in a hurry, Denny had slipped him some rotgut, and that still didn't sit right with Fargo.

He smiled. "Got any *good* whiskey, Denny?"

The men at the bar turned, amused.

"All the whiskey is good here, mister," said Denny.

Fargo smiled again. "Good enough to kill a crocodile."

The men at the bar laughed. One man, with a hatchet face and intense black eyes, glanced over from the card table.

"There's good whiskey and there's better," Denny said philosophically. He reached under the counter, brought up a bottle, and filled a glass. Fargo gulped it; it was smooth. He put a gold eagle on the counter. Denny filled the glass and left the bottle.

Fargo felt easy, took a deep breath, then stared at the sign over the mirror behind the bar. IN GOD WE TRUST, it read. EVERYONE ELSE PAYS CASH. The mirror reflected the card players and the men at the bar. The standing men looked okay, not a mean face in the lot, mostly hard-working wranglers.

At the card table he began to watch, particularly, two men. One was a young husky the players called Matty, wearing a big stetson, and under it was a good-looking, spoiled-kid face, flushed with booze. Surprisingly, most of the chips were in front of him. Opposite sat a man someone called Bronco, hard dark eyes, a hatchet face, a rawboned body. The players handled him carefully, which seemed smart to Fargo; he looked mean, fast, dangerous. It surprised him that Matty kept throwing darts at Bronco, who was losing and didn't like it. Matty was winning, and like an idiot kid, he crowed as if it were not luck but only his skill that kept winning the pots.

Fargo lifted his glass. If that spoiled brat didn't put a cork in his mouth, he might run into a lead wall. Well, a man has a right to his own funeral.

He turned and looked at Denny, who came over. "Know a man called Terry?" Fargo's voice was low.

Denny stared. "Terry Larrabee?"

"And who's he?"

Denny leaned forward, speaking in a low voice. "You gotta be from a long way off. Terry Larrabee is Mr. Big in this territory. The biggest spread, the biggest herd. The Larrabee ranch has three big brothers. And that kid at the card table's the youngest one, Matty."

Fargo turned to look. When he had come into the saloon, Matty had shown no recognition. Matty seemingly didn't know him from a hole in the wall, he'd bet his bottom dollar. So, Terry was Mr. Big around here. That made it even more of a riddle.

Just then Bronco grunted and laid out three aces. His grunt was disappointment because his pot was small. It ate his heart out that when he had a good hand, nobody stayed to challenge.

Matty laughed with gusto. "That's a stinking pot for three aces, Bronco."

The black eyes glared in the lean hatchet face and then Bronco growled in his throat, raking in the chips. Fargo, watching, grew alert. Bronco knew the pot was small, didn't need to be told by a snot-nose Larrabee who was pulling family rank. The kind of brat who liked to slingshot dogs and got a big laugh from it, Fargo thought. The brat

33

probably felt protected by the power of the family. If Bronco got riled, he'd be a hard slugger and a fast gun, Fargo felt. But Matty might know what he could get away with. Still, he was drinking hard, and that made a man stupid.

A few pots later, in a showdown, Bronco bluffed and Matty beat him with a pair of tens. The pot took everything that Bronco had.

Matty pulled in the chips and grinned. "You see, Bronco, you don't need a big, big hand to win. Just a itty-bitty better than the sucker."

"You teaching me, boy? You're still wet behind the ears."

Matty flushed. He'd been drinking plenty and his fogged brain didn't know when he might reach a dangerous edge.

"Maybe wet behind the ears. But who's got the money, Bronco?"

Bronco looked sullen. "A streak of dumb luck. Even a clunk can win with lucky cards."

Fargo, watching, felt that Bronco had probably been sitting on his anger only because Matty was a Larrabee.

Matty, flushed with booze and conceit, leaned back in his chair, shook his head condescendingly. "That's what the loser always says. Beat by dumb luck. Cards is a head game, Bronco, and I gotta say this: you may be fast with a gun, but you're slow in the head."

There was a thud of silence.

The silence made Matty aware of his insult, because for the first time he looked worried.

Fargo, watching Bronco, knew it was too late.

Bronco slowly pushed his chair back, his eyes like molten marbles.

"You son of a bitch Larrabees think you own

34

the world. Can say anything you like. I'm calling you on that." He stood and backed off.

All the men at the table but one scrambled for the walls, as did the men at the bar. Fargo held his position.

Matty sat still, pale as a sheet, and sweat started to glisten on his forehead. He knew that he was no match for Bronco, that he was practically dead.

The man who stayed at the table must have had some connection with the Larrabees. "Don't do it, Bronco. He's just a dumb kid. And you'll have Terry all over you."

"To hell with Terry," Bronco raged. "This half-assed cowboy's been riding my tail all through the game. I took a bellyful. Now I'm taking him. I'm telling you, Charley, step aside."

Charley stood up slowly and walked to the wall.

Matty sat frozen, his face pasty, his eyes wild with fear. "Bronco, I'm sorry. I guess it was the booze. I don't want to mix with you."

Bronco stared hard, then his lip curled with contempt. He was slow to anger, but when it happened, he was unforgiving.

"So you're yellow-bellied, too. It won't help. Stand up."

The silence was deafening.

To everyone it looked like slaughter.

"Hold it, Bronco," Fargo said coolly. It was like a thunderbolt hit the saloon; all eyes turned on him.

Bronco was amazed, then he clenched his teeth.

Fargo smiled at Bronco. "The fella did speak out of turn. But he's apologized. He made a mistake. Be a big man, Bronco and let it pass."

Bronco's rawboned body went rigid for only a

moment. He had a rage for killing and nobody was going to stop him.

"Who the hell are you, mister, telling me what to do? Keep out of it or I'll blow your head off too!"

A heavy moment of silence when nothing moved, the only sound the dull click of the grandfather clock on the wall. Then Fargo slowly moved from the bar, facing Bronco, his eyes diamond points of fire.

They stared at each other, an overwhelming moment when everyone in the room knew one man stood an instant away from death.

Then they moved, and those watching Fargo saw his hand in a blur because of its speed. His bullet ripped into Bronco, splitting his chest open, and the blood gushed. He tottered back, his face showing not pain but amazement, his eyes rooted on Fargo; then his gun fired into the floor and he went down slowly, like a toppled tree, lay there, his body heaving for a few moments. Then he died.

Everyone stood frozen, staring at Bronco, top gun in the territory until just a minute ago. Then they turned, looked at Fargo silently.

Fargo picked up his drink and finished it.

Matty, still pasty white, was stunned, gazed at Bronco, thinking it might be him dead if not for this stranger. He struggled to his feet, still shaky, walked to Fargo, put out his hand.

"I think you just saved my hide, mister. I'm Matty Larrabee. May I buy you a drink?"

Fargo smiled. Perhaps the brat wasn't all bad, though he'd acted like a horse's ass. But he didn't deserve killing for that. Fargo had stepped in not only to stop a useless killing, but because a live Matty Larrabee could help him reach Terry

Larrabee. A plan formed in his mind as he watched the game, and it hadn't included knocking off Matty!

They drank together, and then Matty told Denny to set up drinks for everyone. A couple of men took Bronco's body out, and the card game went on with new players. Ten minutes later, the bar looked just as peaceful as it had before the gunfight.

The color had come back into Matty's face, but he still sounded shaky. "I'll tell you, mister, that last minute, before you stepped in, when I looked at Bronco, I was looking right into my grave. Couldn't beat Bronco in a thousand tries. He's beat the best in this territory." Matty shook his head. "I was crazy drunk to ride him." He looked strangely at Fargo. "If I was a churchgoing man, I'd think somebody up there sent you along to save my skin. What's the name?"

"No point in saying Fargo; it might ring a bell. "Clancy Brown," he fabricated.

"Are you staying awhile in Spoon River?"

Fargo stroked his chin. "I might stay awhile if I found something I liked."

Matty smiled broadly. He wanted to do something to show the power of his family to this stranger.

"I'm sure we can do something, Clancy. The Larrabees swing weight in this county. Come out to our spread, the Bar-L. Terry, he's my oldest brother, will be glad to do something for you. 'Specially when I tell him you outgunned Bronco. He likes a fast gun. I'll have to play down how dumb I was. You understand." He sighed. "When I drink, I get into trouble. My wife's always telling me that." He hitched his belt and finished off his glass. "Are you interested? I'm heading out now."

Fargo nodded. "Maybe I'll mosey out your way tomorrow."

Matty smiled. "Anytime." He put out his hand, and the brown eyes in his broad face gleamed. Fargo walked Matty out of the saloon, watched him swing over the powerful gelding he'd noticed earlier. Matty waved. "Come out tomorrow. It's the second fork on the west trail." And with the high spirits of a young man given a reprieve on life, he whipped his hat on the haunches of the gelding and yelled, "Git goin'!"

Fargo watched him leave and then felt a letdown. He'd eat, get a room, and think about what to do. It didn't seem smart just now to go out to the ranch, where Terry was surrounded by brothers and probably a gang of ranch hands. Like going into the lion's den. He'd have to work out a plan.

He stabled the pinto, and walked to the hotel: a two-story, white-framed building with a large dining room. He ate a fine thick steak, home-fried potatoes, two ears of buttered corn, and finished with pumpkin pie and coffee. It felt good to eat like that after the monotonous diet of the trail. He climbed up to the room, peeled off his clothes, looked out of the window at the night sky. It glittered with a million silver stars and gave him an awesome sense of mystery. He lay on the bed, surprisingly soft, and looked at the sky, his eyes heavy. Tomorrow he'd think more about Terry, a man who wanted him dead. Fargo didn't take kindly to that. On that thought, sleep hit him like a ton of bricks.

* * *

The sun glared through the open window and he was jarred to realize a good piece of morning was gone. He had dreamed the sound of bells, and now, awake, he realized it was the real thing, coming from a nearby church.

About fifty yards away, he could see from his window the freshly painted white church, with horses and buggies clustered around.

In the dining room he ate a thick cut of fried ham, scrambled eggs, several biscuits, and drank two cups of coffee. It put the perk back in him. He went out to a porch set back from the street, slouched deep in a beat-up armchair. The sun hit down hard and he slipped his hat to eye level and thought of the Larrabees.

Yes, Matty could be the pass to the Larrabee ranch, but was it smart to confront Terry there? Much easier to nail him in town than fight through a gang of brothers and ranch hands.

Not to reveal his name had been a good move. If Matty told his brother Terry that a man named Fargo just knocked off Bronco, Terry would send a posse. Still a damned riddle why Terry wanted his hide.

Church was over and people drifted past, some on foot, some on horse or buggy. The women wore calico and bonnets, men their best duds.

Two prancing horses came by pulling a shiny black buggy. In it the elegant woman he'd seen on the road, now in a silky black dress that her white flesh filled with sexy curves. He came alert, and her dark black eyes swiveled to him, and again a secret smile twisted the corners of her mouth. She's a fancy looker, he thought, and not suffering money trouble.

He slouched down again, the hat back to eye level, his legs stretched out. Minutes later he stiffened as two spirited black horses came by pulling another buggy. Three familiar faces were in it: Abigail, Maude, and Julia. As the horses cantered past the porch, the women caught sight of him, and shock hit them all; they exchanged glances. Abigail turned to look at him, and her cobalt-blue eyes drilled into his, though her face stayed a mask.

Then came three men, each on a great-looking horse, clearly escort to the women's buggy. There were two redheads, one with huge shoulders, a thick neck, and arms like hams. The second man was a slightly smaller version. The third man was Matty Larrabee. They thudded past in a hurry. Fargo watched until they faded out of sight, then leaned back and grimaced. This didn't add up. The three women—and no doubt about it—belonged to the three men. And the men were brothers, and all were Larrabees. Now, why in hell would these women—women with men like that, hard, tough, red-blooded—go out looking for sex on the trail? There couldn't be anything wrong with those guys. They'd be ripsnorters about whiskey and women. And such men didn't share what they owned, either.

He took off his hat and scratched his head as a hard thought hit him. Somehow Terry must have found out the Larrabee women had pitched a tumble with a man named Fargo and sent his killers to the big oak to track and kill him.

Why? To protect family pride? Jealousy? Terry didn't know him from a brick wall, but wanted him eliminated.

Fargo clapped his hat back on his head, walked to the end of the porch, and stared at two elm trees growing at the side of the hotel. But he didn't clearly see them. He was still thinking too hard of the Larrabee women.

Why'd they do it? Why pick him? It was one hell of a puzzle. He'd been sleeping under a tree, the women put a gun on him, forced him into sex. Then their men put a pack of killers on his trail.

He didn't like it. Not a bit of it. It was good that he used the name "Clancy Brown." Now he could ride out to the ranch with Matty's blessing and see if he could smoke out some answers.

Of course it was dangerous, riding bold into the enemy camp. Any one of the women could break his cover. But wouldn't it be stupid for them to do that? Still, it could happen. It was all a barrel of snakes.

But the one thing that bothered him most was that Terry Larrabee wanted him dead.

Yes, a little later he'd ride out to the ranch and get some answers. It'd be like tiptoeing on gunpowder.

But there was another lure: Abigail. Wasn't she unfinished business?

3

Before starting for the Larrabee ranch, Fargo
looked the pinto over carefully. He always did
this before he left town, where, in case of a
problem, he could find a smithy. Sometimes it
seemed he took better care of the Ovaro than of
himself. He could never put into words his feelings about the pinto and would find it hard to
forgive himself if, because he had been careless,
the horse went lame on the trail. The bond between them was deep, emotional. He loved the
horse. And the horse sensed his moods, and in
time of danger his loyalty was such he'd run his
heart out for Fargo.

In this checkout, Fargo found the shoe on the
right foreleg beginning to loosen. He took the
horse to the smithy, a man called Judd, who in a
few minutes time, put on a new shoe. Judd, a
short brawny man with a red face and light blue
eyes, said nothing until he finished. Then he
pulled out a pipe and tobacco pouch from behind
his leather apron and looked shrewdly at Fargo.

"I heard what happened at Denny's. Never
thought the day would come when the Bronco
would go down."

Fargo patted the haunches of the pinto, but
said nothing.

Judd stroked his chin. "I saw Bronco against

the Dakota Kid. The kid had a big rep, but Bronco moved like lightning." He shook his head. "I s'pose, sooner or later, there's always someone out there jest a touch faster."

Fargo laughed. "I hope I don't meet that guy." He took a golden eagle from his leather pouch. "What do you know about Terry Larrabee?"

The smith puffed his pipe reflectively, "Terry? A rawhide man. He runs that ranch with an iron fist. It was the old man Larrabee who made the Larrabee the big L. After he died, Terry has tried to keep it big. He's been hard and shrewd, but he's not as smart as the old man. He's got more horses than he can feed. And the government ain't buying horses now." Judd paused. "You thinking of offering your services, Mr. Brown?"

"I just might." Fargo pulled the pinto out of the shed, swung over the saddle. "Think I'll mosey out and take a look."

Though the sun struck down hard, it was not the scorcher of two days ago. Fargo let the pinto move at its own pace, no point sweating it. He looked at the land with its steep rises and slopes, the stretch of lush green. In the distance the great mountain range climbed up, surrounded by a simmering purplish haze. The trail twisted and turned and sometimes went treacherous with stones that rolled from the steep hill alongside. The pinto picked its way, and as Fargo rounded a sharp turn, he stared in astonishment—the shiny, elegant buggy he'd seen twice before was now lying on its side, one wheel off, looking like a wounded spider. A brawny cowboy with a craggy nose was scowling at it. Nearby, the flashy, big-breasted woman in her silky black dress looked cross. "Staring at the wheel, Nosey, ain't going to make it rise up and fix to the wagon. Do something."

"But I can't lift the wagon myself, Miss Ruby."

They heard Fargo then and turned, the lady giving him a slow smile. "Can you help a lady in trouble, mister?"

Fargo swung off the pinto.

She had fair skin, black eyes, a Cupid's-bow mouth, and lush auburn hair that curled to her shoulders. Her breasts were white, and the low-cut dress revealed a hell of a pair. She'd be a shameless hussy, he thought, if she didn't look so damned prosperous. That buggy must have cost a fortune, with its shiny black wood, leather riggings, slim wheels painted black and trimmed with gold. And those prancing grays, with their graceful lines, looked almost worth their weight in coin.

"This buggy, as you can see, has gone and thrown its wheel. Can you think of some way to help."

Fargo grimaced. The wheel had been bent at the rim when it was sprung from the wagon. "You'll need the smith to get that wheel right, miss," he said.

She scowled, stared at him thoughtfully, then turned to Nosey. "Why in hell did you want to lift the wagon when the wheel was no good?" she demanded.

Nosey scratched his big chin and looked embarrassed.

She turned back to Fargo. "My name is Ruby Carson. I'm in a hurry to get to my place. It's just three miles. Once I get there, I'll send some men out to help Nosey. But I have to get there fast."

"You could use one of your grays," he suggested.

"No. They're prancers. I don't want to use the grays." She gazed at him. "What about you?"

He smiled. "What about me?"

Her look was direct and bold. "I could ride with you."

He nodded. "You could."

She was a good-looking woman and he didn't mind doing a favor. Her dress was long, and she'd look ridiculous on horseback, but it didn't seem to matter to her.

"What's your name, mister?"

"Clancy, Clancy Brown."

She looked at him sharply, then turned to the driver. "I'll go with him, Nosey, and send Spud and Bill out to help you. You give me a hand up on his horse."

She stepped on the hands Nosey put together and swung one black-stockinged leg over the horse, put her arms around Fargo's waist. Her full woman's body pressed against his back, and the heat went through him. He could feel her breasts, firm and big, pushing against him, and her belly and thighs. Something about her body sizzled, and as he started off, it took an effort of will to pull his mind from her and look at the trail.

The powerful pinto, though loaded with two burdens, still moved easily.

"There's a turn off about a mile ahead. It leads to my place." Her round white arms held his waist tightly, and as they rode, the canter of the horse jarred her interlocked hands so that, by chance, they slipped down and brushed against his bulge. At first when it happened, she moved away, though not too quickly. Later, she moved away slower.

"So you're Clancy Brown. The man who planted Bronco in boot hill."

"Word gets around fast in Spoon River."

"It gets to me fast," she said. "There isn't much that goes on that I don't know."

"Are you in business?"

"I own some land. A lady has to look out for herself."

"You must do pretty good. That buggy looks special."

"Had it shipped from Chicago. I don't like to ride. It's not ladylike."

He smiled. She wasn't his idea of a lady. But she sounded plenty shrewd. Probably got a grip on land with water and leased it out to surrounding landowners.

They rode in silence.

"Where were you headed?" she asked.

"Thought I might look things over at the Larrabee ranch."

"The Larrabee ranch. They'll love you there. You saved Matty from a hole in the head. He's got a mean mouth. Only Terry can keep a lid on it. Have you met him?"

"Who?"

"Terry Larrabee."

"No. What's he like?"

She was silent a long time. He wished he could see her face. He sensed a big current of feeling.

"Terry's a bull. He's proud. Doesn't want anyone soiling the family name. All the Larrabees are like that. Luke is the biggest, built like the side of a house. He's the foreman. They run horses and it's not a good time. Matty is the runt. Always in trouble. He's fast shooting with his mouth, slow on the draw. Not like you. I can tell. You talk slow and shoot fast. And you've got a body hard as iron." Then she laughed. "A hard-on like iron, too."

He stared ahead, aware that his body had re-acted to her closeness. Her body felt hot as fire against him, and her firm big breasts kept bump-ing into him. She was one sexy lady, and he wondered if he'd be able to make it all the way to her place without a pass. What made it tough were her movements. She pressed hard against him; he could smell her perfume, and it was fancy and sexy. She was aware that he was ri-ding erect, which seemed to amuse her. And it seemed to do plenty to her. Her last remark was bold and brassy.

They were approaching a thick grove of trees and bushes, and it was then, as if by accident, that her hands slipped down again to the bulge in his britches, and this time they stayed there. The ache in his loins was painful. The lady was asking for it, and he felt hard enough to nail her to the ground. When they came to the thicket, he left the trail, found a narrow passage, and put the pinto through it. The thick growth of bushes and trees made it very private.

"Lost your way, Clancy?" she said. But her hands were planted firmly on his britches, under which seethed massive excitement.

"I think we found it," he said.

"We?"

"Yes." With a quick expert move, he unleashed his physical excitement and then brought her hands back around it.

She was silent for a moment.

"You *are* big," she said, her voice husky and low.

Then he swung away from the pinto, lifted her off, and she fell in a sitting position, he standing in front of her, his sex flaming and pulsating.

Her eyes gleamed; she seemed hypnotized.

Then, without a word, she moved her face close to it, pressed it against her cheeks, rubbed it against her lips, and suddenly her Cupid's-bow mouth opened. It was a moment of anguished pleasure for him, and he looked down. Her tension spiraled as her mouth moved as if with insatiable hunger, reaching into the pit of her body. He felt an irresistible desire to thrust deep into her, but held off while she did extraordinary things to him, showing amazing skill. Finally, pushed by an unendurable urge to pierce her, he gently pushed her back to the grass, reached under her silky black dress, pulled off her undergarment, and pulled down on her dress so that one of her breasts jumped out. He stared at the pink nipple against the snowy-white flesh, let his tongue work over it, filling his mouth, then reaching down with his hand to between her thighs, feeling the moist lush flesh. He turned her so that her creamy mounds were on top, then spread them and slid between them into the warm crease. Then he began to work in and out, thrusting, each one a moment of marvelous pleasure. His flesh felt fierce, almost ironlike, as he thrust it in rhythm.

She whimpered, whispered, and seemed lost in her own world of sensations. And so it went, on and on, and every so often her body would tighten, as if she were branded by a hot iron, then she'd loosen, and he'd hit her again and again, and she moaned and moaned; and finally he felt tension collect in a moment of intolerable pleasure, then he exploded. She flung herself against him in a frenzy of movement, and he felt her pulsations run on and on. He slumped over her. As part of his mind moved away, he had to admit that this Ruby, whom he didn't know, didn't care for, probably might never see again, had been one of the best rides ever. It had been low-down physical passion, and the very best.

It was about a mile to her place, and until they reached it, they scarcely spoke two sentences. She had a big white house on land that went out flat, then sloped down to a fair-sized stream. Two hired hands came out of the house, looking curiously at him. He slipped off the pinto, helped her down. She turned to the men. "The buggy's down with Nosey, a mile out. Go help him."

After they left, she turned to him. Her liquid black eyes glowed with feeling. "Why don't you stay here? You'll like it."

He shook his head. "I told Matty that I would drop by."

She studied him. "You're a tumbleweed. Nothing nails a man like you down, does it? Not a place, not a woman. I can tell. It's a pity. Because you sure can make a woman happy."

He grinned. "It's been real friendly. I'll see you around, Ruby." He swung over the horse, wheeled it, and started for the trail.

4

The sun was still high by the time he reached the Larrabee ranch, a giant spread, reaching as far as the eye could see. And he rode smack into a bang-up, rip-roaring game of bronco-busting. The wranglers, at least fifteen, were hanging on the fence of a corral where the wildest-eyed stallion he ever saw leaped, jumped, humped its back, and threw its rider fifteen feet through the air. A roar went up. The stallion, having dumped the rider, just stood motionless, like a statue.

It was comic and Fargo smiled. A giant of a man in a big stetson had turned to look at him, as did the other men, but their attention shot back to the stallion as another brave rider approached it. The giant, who Fargo thought would be Luke Larrabee, stayed curious and came toward him.

Fargo swung off the horse. "Clancy Brown," he said.

The big man had shrewd gray eyes in a face that looked carved from rock, a wide thin mouth, all this perched on a bull neck. His body, too, looked massive and rock-hard. Not the kind of man you'd want to tackle in a one-to-one brawl, Fargo thought.

"Clancy Brown." His voice rumbled from the big chest. "I heard you knocked off Bronco. That's shooting." He grinned. "Not sure you did us a favor, saving Matty's tail. It's a miracle that block-head is still alive. Always shooting off his mouth." He put out his hand, a huge mass of meat and knuckles. "You look like a good-sized fella. Interested in hanging on for a while?"

"Might be," Fargo said.

A shout turned their attention to the stallion. Two men were holding it while the new rider threw a leg over it. The men holding let go and sprinted for the fence. The rider, hefty, with blond, curly hair, broad shoulders, and a smirk on his broad-boned face, yelled, "Git, git, you mangy polecat!"

The stallion stood immovable as stone. There was silence. The rider slapped hard against the rump, yelled again. Nothing. Then, like a lightning bolt, the horse moved. He jumped, his back humped about six feet, came down hard, kicked, bumped, doubled up, sprinted like it had seen the devil, stopped suddenly on a dime, heaved its back, and sent the rider crashing against the fence. The horse then trotted to the center and stood still, like a stone statue.

Luke Larrabee, smiling, shook his head. "We call him Black Lightning. Nobody can break him. Even come near. Whenever we get a dull spell, we bring him out and a couple of men interested in suicide try him."

Fargo studied the horse. Nobody would dream that quiet animal could, within three seconds, turn into a snorting, stampeding, ornery tangle of horseflesh. He didn't like man or a weight on his back. He wanted to be free and running and doing his favorite thing with the mares. If he had to stay penned up by this queer, two-footed animal who kept him from his natural life, running free, he would never submit. He would destroy either the man or himself.

Fargo, as he studied Black Lightning, was trying to reach into his mind. The horse didn't know yet that, as its master, man could give him a good life, protect him from hunger, thirst, disease, the harshness of nature.

Luke, watching him, smiled. "I hope, Clancy, you're not thinking what I think you're thinking."

Fargo laughed. "I never met a horse or a woman that couldn't be tamed."

Luke laughed too. "That's a funny thing to say, but I'll pass it by. I wouldn't want the man who saved Matty to get paid off with a broken leg."

"I like the challenge," Fargo said. At that moment, a door opened in the big house, and two women came out, walked to horses tethered to posts nearby. They mounted and directed the horses toward the corral.

Abigail and Julia, Fargo noted, in cowgirl hats, smart leather dresses, and boots. He couldn't for the moment help thinking of Julia's naked flesh, her big breasts, and himself inside. It was a flash moment, and aware of the danger, he made his face expressionless. But Luke had followed his glance and glimpsed something, not that he clearly understood it, but he didn't like it. Julia might be his woman, or if not, she belonged to a Larrabee. A subtle shift seemed to happen to Luke, a flash of anger, then a new craftiness.

"Of course," he drawled, "if you're the kind of man who likes a challenge, who likes to tame every women and horse he meets, then I suppose I ought to let you try Black Lightning." He pushed the big hat back on his head. "Might be a good show. I'll tell the men."

Fargo watched him walk to the fence. The men turned abruptly to stare at him.

They want to see what a ten-carat nut looks like, Fargo thought. He walked toward the corral. Julia, probably off on some errand in town, rode toward the gate of the ranch, but Abigail brought her horse to the fence, to watch. By this time, word had spread, and cowboys piled out of the bunkhouse so that the fence was crowded with men curious about the stranger who set himself up for slaughter.

The stallion, though standing quietly, was held by two men. Fargo came slowly toward its head, so that the stallion could clearly see him. He could read in the big black eyes hate and distrust, another two-footed enemy out to destroy his spirit. A ripple passed over the muscular body, the only sign of its inner tension.

"After I get on, move fast, move out," he said to the men. He waited until they cleared the corral, then talked in a gentle voice to the horse, looking directly into its eyes.

The stallion had heard lots of voices and was ready to disregard this one. But the voice went on and on, soothing, soft. The man stood there, his eyes gentle, his touch soft, caressing. A different man, but still a two-footed devil, out to humble, hurt, and destroy. He'd play dumb, as he did with the others; then, when this hated two-footed animal tried to climb on its back, he would throw him into the wind, like the others.

The man now put his hand on his flesh, and he felt his flesh crawl at the touch. Man, the enemy. Yet his touch was soft, gentle. He was different, yet the same. For he already moved close to jump on this hated burden they had tied to his back and under his belly, which he could not shake off. But he could shake the man, kick him, throw him into the sky.

The man moved close. Like the others, he'd let him climb on his back, then he'd jump, and this one, too, would fly through the air and crash to the earth like a stone.

Now he felt the man, an intolerable weight. The man talked gently, he stroked, but it would do no good. He stopped listening. Now! He flung himself in a great hump into the air, came down on stiff legs, he bucked, he bumped, he shot forward, stopped, braced his legs and heaved. Nothing. The hated man burden was still on his back! Unthinkable! He bucked, squirmed in the air, twisted, turned, kicked, shot out like a bullet, stopped suddenly, pawed at the sky, trying to shake off the hateful burden. If only he could turn and tear with his teeth the creature that had become part of him.

He could hear the other two-legged creatures on the fence yelling, waving their hats. It was a horror, the worst of all things, but he could not throw off this one. Nothing he did worked; the man stayed on. He could taste blood, his lungs were bursting, his heart was thundering, but he could do nothing more; his strength was going, he felt himself weakening. There was nothing he could do. It was defeat, a terrible defeat. The two-legged creature had stayed on and he would have to live with it. Such a man as this one could not be beat. And yet, he had not been cruel, he had not hurt, he had been gentle. Perhaps it would not be the end of life if he let the man ride. Perhaps. The hands gently turned him right, and he moved right, to the fence; then, following the gentle guide of the hands, he trotted around the fence. The two-legged creatures were roaring, smiling, whistling, but it didn't matter anymore.

He had lost his battle with this one man.

It would never be the same.

Fargo couldn't help but smile at the wranglers, hanging on the fence, the way they went wild. They had seen one bronco-buster after the other bite the dust, dumped by Black Lightning, and they despaired that any rider could tame its unbreakable spirit. It had been accomplished, finally, by this lean, powerful stranger who just mounted up and did it. And that demon horse had never kicked its devil heels more viciously.

Fargo grinned as they shook his hand, clapped his back. He understood that, to them, it stood for a victory of man over beast, by man over the untamable. All the men there, he thought, participated in his win over the stubborn brute.

Luke's response was more subdued, and the gleam in his eye more wary, as if, Fargo thought, he had discovered something in the stranger that made him more dangerous. Luke's gray eyes locked on his. "I reckon, Clancy, you were not braggin' about taming horse and woman."

Fargo laughed. "Easier to tame a horse than a woman, Luke."

Luke did not smile. "I don't think you'd get much trouble from the women." Luke looked toward Abigail, still sitting on her horse at the other end of the corral, from where she had watched the bronco-busting. Luke was trying to read her face, but even to Fargo it was a mask without expression.

She prodded her horse, a graceful sorrel, toward them, and Luke's broad face looked grim. He waited until she reached them. "This is

Abigail. She's Matty's wife. This is Clancy Brown. He saved Matty's skin yesterday in town. From Bronco. I s'pose you heard."

"I heard." She had a small smile. "So it was you who did it. We're mighty thankful." She was cool, smiling, and better than ever to look at with that graceful body, all the curves in the right place, and that saucy mouth and those cobalt eyes that held steady on his. It wasn't hard to sense the whirl of thoughts behind them.

Luke was shrewdly studying them. Then he said, "Clancy may stick with us for a time. Why not show him the place, Abigail? Unless you had some errand in mind."

"Nothing that can't be put aside, Luke. I'll be glad to show Mr. Brown around."

"Call him Clancy," Luke said. "After all, Abigail, you wouldn't have Matty to keep you warm on cold nights if it wasn't for Clancy."

She didn't smile, but just prodded her horse, and Fargo, after a wave at Luke, followed after. He felt Luke's eyes on his back. The man's body might be big as a house, but his brain wasn't small.

The sun had started down and a light breeze brought with it the smell of June grass. The Bar-L ranch was a huge tract of land with valleys, slopes, hills. They passed great corrals of horses. Abigail didn't say a word, just rode silently until they were miles from the ranch house, the bunks, and the corrals. They came near a rising formation of rocks that connected to a great range of mountain that stretched west. When they reached a rill, she swung off her horse and let it drink. He turned the pinto loose. She was sitting on a grassy knoll and looked at him.

"What the hell's the idea, Fargo?"

"What idea?" He wasn't going to make it easy.

She bit her lip and it was easy to see she had bottled up hard feelings. "I asked you to keep riding, not to come back to Spoon River. Not only did you come back, you made the terrible mistake of coming here."

"Is it a terrible mistake?"

"It's that, all right."

"Why?"

"Because if Terry or Luke discovers who you are, you won't last a minute."

"And are you going to tell them?"

Her saucy mouth firmed. "I don't yet know what I'm going to do." She took off her hat, and the sun hit her blond hair so that it glowed.

He picked a blade of grass, stared at it. "Let me tell you, Abigail, what I'm going to do."

"Yes, tell that."

"I'm going to find out why Terry sent three killers after me."

That jolted her. "He did what?"

"You heard me."

Her pretty face was serious. She took a deep breath. "I'm sorry to hear that. I had no idea he would go that far."

"How'd it happen?"

She looked at the mountains. "I don't know."

"Oh, you know, all right. You know it all. And you're going to tell it all."

She turned, her face now grim. "So that's why you came back."

"Yes. I don't care about being a target for gunslingers. So, talk." His voice rasped.

A strange smile came to her wide-lipped mouth. "S'pose I don't talk."

His jaw hardened. "I think you will."

"Are you threatening me? With what?"

His tone was hard. "I always felt you'd be the best of the three. But never had the chance to find out. I could find out now—if you force me."

"If you tried that, you'd never leave this ranch alive."

"You never know," he said.

She looked again to the range, and he found her profile fascinating. If she didn't deliver, he'd just as soon bear down on her. His life was on the line and he had to know why.

After a long silence, her blue eyes met his. "I suppose you have a right to know. Ask your questions."

"First. Why did you women pull guns on me for sex. All of you married. To red-blooded men."

Her mouth curled. "Those red-blooded men were being too red-blooded with Miss Ruby Carson, a bitch who lives some miles from here. She's put a spell on them. Maude and Julia didn't like it. They wanted revenge." She smiled. "It was a problem of finding someone not too repulsive, a stranger passing through. They didn't want the man killed. You seemed right. Much better-looking than we expected." She grimaced. "They didn't expect you to be such a hotshot lover."

"And why didn't you get into it?"

She shrugged. "I didn't want to. I don't care what Matty does. Not anymore. He was a mistake. Much worse, in fact. Just between us, I'm not all that glad you stopped Bronco from dropping Matty." Her voice was harsh.

He nodded slowly. So that's why it all happened. It was beginning to make sense. Maude and Julia, with this twisted idea of revenge, picked on a stranger passing through to strike back at their disloyal husbands.

"So, after it happened, they told the Larrabee brothers?" he asked.

"Of course. How else would it be revenge?"

"They told Terry a man called Fargo was involved?"

"Oh, Terry got real nasty with Maude, and got it from her, the name, where it happened. He had no idea who Fargo was, but told his gunslingers to pick up your tracks at the great oak. The rest you know."

Fargo was silent, aware of intense light in those cool blue eyes.

"What was it? Family honor? Male pride? That sort of thing. Did he send his killers to avenge the family honor?"

"Some of both," she said.

It was just as he'd guessed. "What'd they do to the women?"

"Roughed them up. But not badly." She looked away. "They felt some guilt, after all, about Ruby." She put her hat over her golden hair. "If I were you, Fargo, I'd clear out of here fast as the wind. It's a death trap."

He'd been in a lot of death traps, he thought. "Are you going to talk?"

"No. Not I."

"The others?"

"Who knows about the others? We're women. We're called the unpredictable sex. Right?"

In his experience, most people blabbed when they knew something. "I'll leave when it's right. Terry will begin to wonder what happened to his gunslingers. And to Fargo."

Her smile was taut. "It may be too late."

He shrugged. Her fine breasts pushed against her shirt. "It's a shame. You don't like Matty, but you won't step outside for fun."

"It's like that. I don't break vows. But I'll get out, sooner or later. You'd never think it to look at him, but Matty has a vicious streak."

"Perhaps I can help."

Her smile was strange. "You're too helpful. I want to get back to my home town, Fremont. But Matty can be a mean bastard. Doesn't let go easy." She swung over her horse. "Meanwhile, if I were you, I'd be extremely careful. You're in the lion's mouth right now."

"I'll be careful. Just let me know if you want me for anything." He grinned.

"By the way," she said before starting out, "what happened to those killers Terry sent after you?"

"I'm here and they're not," he said.

She stared at him. "You're good with guns, with horses, and with women. What else are you good with, Fargo?"

He smiled. "But you don't know, Abigail, if I'm good with women. You just have someone's word for it. Why not find out for yourself?"

She shook her head. "I told you, you're in the lion's mouth. You don't seem to realize it." She spurred her horse.

He followed her slowly. It was true. There were at least twenty-five men ready to do anything Terry wanted. And the last thing he should be thinking about was women. But he had found that danger gave more spice to the women thing. And Abigail was a prize worth pursuing.

He put the pinto into a canter.

By the time they reached the ranch, the sun had slid to the horizon and the sky was flame-yellow. The men were in the bunkhouses, and from one the sound of a guitar floated out, a sad tune, Fargo thought.

As they hitched their horses to the post near the big white house, Luke came out, big and hulking, alongside a redheaded man. This had to be Terry, a smaller version of Luke, Fargo thought. He had the same solid bone frame, but with finer features, a more commanding presence; his eyes were gray and piercing, and just now they raked his face, his body, then swung over to Abigail, as if to read what he could there. Her face wore a mask.

He put out his hand. "Clancy Brown. It's a pleasure, pardner. I hear Abigail's been showing you the place. What do you think of it? A showplace, eh? Like Abigail here. She's a show-piece, too." He grinned with honest lust. "If only I had met Abigail before Maude, things would be different around here. It's a pity."

Abigail did not smile. "It's a pity that I met Matty altogether." She turned and walked into a side-door entrance of the big house.

Fargo noticed that they all watched her, and he smiled: everyone likes to watch a beautiful woman move.

Terry had an ugly look. "That goddamned Matty spoils everything he touches." Then he turned to Fargo, his manner easy. "I heard what happened at Denny's. Got a blow-by-blow description. Not from Matty. To hear him, you'd never think that spoiled brat ever did a wrong thing. We're always pulling him outta the line of fire. This time, nobody could have done it. Not against Bronco. But you did it. I gotta hand it to you, Clancy. You gotta be faster than greased lightning. C'mon into the house."

As they walked toward the big house, Fargo

tried to figure Terry. His voice oozed friendliness, but those piercing eyes were cold as frozen marbles. You didn't let your guard down with this sort of man.

It took money to build a house like this: an enormous living room with lush rugs, a long pinewood table, two divans, and several easy chairs, a mahogany bureau with many bottles of liquor, fancy pictures on the walls.

Luke didn't waste a moment, but broke open a bottle and filled three shot glasses.

Terry lifted his. "To your health, Clancy Brown. You're the fastest gun in this territory."

Fargo drank, then he said, "A man is fast until he meets someone faster. Then he's as dead as the slowest man in the cemetery."

Terry laughed. "Don't worry about a thing, Clancy. Bronco was practically a legend hereabouts. Never beat in a draw, not in years. Now you'll be the legend. You won't have to draw."

He motioned to Luke, who refilled the glasses. "Once you get a rep, everyone gives you space. Right, Luke?"

Luke, who had stopped smiling, just nodded. "I never wear a gun. I'm the slowest draw in the county."

Terry grinned. "But Luke is the hardest hitter. He once knocked a stubborn mule flat on its ass. Everyone gives Luke space." He leaned forward. "We need men like that on the Larrabee ranch, Clancy. To put the fear of God in other men."

He talks a blue streak, thought Fargo. What the hell's he after? He tossed off his drink.

"Luke tells me that you're looking." Terry leaned back. "Work for me. I'll make it worth your while."

"What work?"

Terry smiled. "Just be here when I need you. Easy work, especially for your talent."

"Doing what?"

Terry signaled Luke, who filled all glasses.

"Listen, Clancy. We got horses. Corrals full. And we got rustlers. Where the honey is, the bear goes. There's a gang of men rustling out of Red Hills. We don't know their hideout. Every once in a while, we grab one, but he won't talk. He'll hang, but won't talk." Terry paused. "You might take a look around. Maybe you'll find something . . ."

Fargo just looked at him. He was not interested in rustlers. What he wanted to know was what Terry would do when he discovered his three gunmen were buried. He needed some pretext to be here when that happened, and one reason was as good as another. He'd go through the motions. Meanwhile, Abigail was here, too.

"What about it, Clancy? Are you with us?"

Fargo stroked his chin. "Why don't I hang on here for a couple of days and see if I like it?"

"Okay, Clancy. You'll like it here. Best grub in miles. Town has a dance Friday nights. Plenty of excitement." He raised his glass and smiled broadly.

Fargo raised his glass, too. He couldn't help wonder in what part of the house Abigail slept.

Luke just watched him with narrowed eyes.

A hired hand named Clem helped Fargo set up in the end bunkhouse. The plain room had a low beamed ceiling, two cots, a battered table, chairs, and a window. Clem, a rangy cowboy with a lined face, brought clean blankets for the cot. A man's clothing hung on the wall pegs.

"Anything you need just yell," said Clem.

"Who's in the other cot?"

"Conway. He bunks here."

"Where's he now?"

"On the trail. Out looking."

Fargo's eyes narrowed. "Looking for what?"

Clem shrugged. "For Scarface Smitty and his two men. They went out on a special for Terry. Shoulda been back by now. Don't look good. That's why Terry sent Conway. To find out. He'll probably find them in a whiskey hole somewheres."

Clem walked to the door, scratched his scraggy chin, and grinned. "That was some ride you gave Black Lightning. That critter busted more bones than you'll find in a graveyard. It was good ridin'." He shook his head, went out the door.

Fargo lay on the cot, hands behind his head. He could see, through the window, the night sky with stars starting to pop out on the light blue. He looked at Conway's clothes.

So the man bunking here, Conway, had been sent on the trail to find three missing gunmen. That made things sticky. What would Conway find? The graves? If he found graves, he'd have to dig. If he dug, he'd report to Terry that his men had been bushwhacked. What would Terry do then?

He tried to get into Terry's mind, but it was hard. Would he forget the whole thing or would he worry? Any man tough enough to knock off his three gunslingers would be a man to worry about.

The key point was this: would he worry that Fargo might come looking for revenge? Fargo gazed at the sky, with its silver lights. He had two points on his side: Terry couldn't know that Fargo discovered who sent the gunmen. And if

Fargo did know, Terry would not believe that Fargo would come to this ranch. That'd be suicide.

So, for the moment, things would be quiet.

When Conway got back, Fargo decided, things might get unquiet.

5

Next morning, after a breakfast of pancakes, eggs, biscuits, and coffee, he rode south. Toward the Red Hills, from where, Terry told him, rustlers came to prey on the Larrabee horses. He'd reconnoiter, not that he cared one damn bit about rustlers or working for Larrabee. Ranch work, or any work on schedule, was the last thing he cared about. He was the Trailsman, liked to be free on the slope on the prairie, to move free as a bird.

It was a clear, cloudless day, and the sky shone with the blue of Abigail's eyes. He became aware that he was being tailed by a woman on a sorrel. He pretended not to notice and she tried to be shifty. But when he turned southeast, she turned to keep him in sight. It was Maude, the lady with the red hair, blue-green eyes, and milk-white body. The one with the snot-nose attitude, the one he had screwed until she turned to jelly, Terry's woman, and he wondered what she wanted. Surely she didn't hope to pull that pistol trick again. No, she'd probably cuss him out for turning up at Bar-L.

He rode toward a maze of boulders, where it should be easy to lose her. As if aware of his intention, she spurred her sorrel forward. He moved deeper into the maze, slipped off the pinto, and waited.

After ten minutes, she found him. He was, by that time, lying on the ground, sprawled out, his head against the boulder. She came in on her sorrel, looked down, then swung off the saddle. She wore riding pants, which her buttocks filled abundantly. For a full minute she stared sternly toward him.

"When Abigail told me you were here, I told her she'd gone a little crazy. But you *are* here."

"In the flesh."

She was wearing a silk blue shirt that gave full play to her breasts, black shining boots over her riding pants. Now she put her hands on her hips. "It's you who's gone a little crazy. Do you know what Terry would do to you if he knew you were here?"

"Tell me."

Her eyes widened at his insolence. She clenched her teeth. "He'd deprive you of that sex article you take so much pride in."

He grinned. "I wonder if I take as much pride in it as you do, Maude."

She flushed, looked off in the distance, then spoke evenly, as if she decided to relax. "Do you intend to stay here?"

He smiled. "Why not? Good grub, good money, pretty women."

"Aren't you afraid that Terry will find out?"

"Would you tell him?"

A strange look came to her eyes. "Who do you suppose told him about you?"

His jaw hardened. "Why'd you do that?"

She looked troubled. "I didn't want to give him your name. Just that I had paid him off for Ruby." She sighed. "That wasn't enough for him. When Terry wants something, you'd better give it to him. That's the Larrabees, a pack of brutes."

He shrugged. "Don't expect sympathy from me. You told him who I was, and he sent three gunmen after me."

"I know." A grudging glint of admiration crept into those blue-green eyes. "You've got a lot of guts, Fargo, to come here after that."

"I don't like anyone shooting at me," he said coldly.

"I don't blame you." She smiled coquettishly. She took a deep breath and her breasts pushed against the silky shirt; she was sending out heat waves.

Fargo gritted his teeth. This bitch indirectly caused the death of three men, almost his own, yet there she was waving her ass at him, playing with the idea that he was going to stud her again. Her brains must be boiled by the sun.

"Fargo," she said, "you see before you a very unhappy woman."

"That breaks my heart."

"My husband just this morning went off to pay court to Miss Ruby Carson. I'd like to know what that woman's got. She's got the other Larrabees too. It's a real mystery. Maybe it's her perfume. I asked Terry not to go. What he said was not polite." Her nostrils widened. "He's disloyal. In fact, he's a rotten cheat. I think that gives me the right to do what I want. Don't you agree, Fargo?"

"Oh, sure, Maude. Find someone. Enjoy yourself."

She laughed. "You've got a sense of humor. I have found someone. Someone twice the lover that Terry is."

"Great. I wish you luck." He stood and stretched, preparing to go to the pinto.

Her pretty face scowled. "You continue to misunderstand me, Fargo. I mean to revenge myself on Terry again. And that means you."

He turned slowly. "Me?"

"That's it. You're not a bad lover, when it comes down to it. And you'll be discreet. Yes, you're the one."

He stared hard. "Let's just say that I'm not in the mood today."

A smile played on her full lips. "I'm disappointed in you. An attractive woman offers herself and you turn away. That's not polite."

He looked at her body. She was stacked like a dream, all right. He remembered her milk-white skin, the taste of her nipples. But he didn't like to be forced into anything, not even into sex, even with a woman like this one.

"I like to pick my shots," he said slowly.

Her blue-green eyes turned frosty. "I like to pick mine, too. And you're it."

His mouth twisted. "What are you going to do? Pull a gun on me again? I'm not asleep this time."

"Oh, I know you're fast. Everyone knows that, but they don't know this: that Fargo and Clancy Brown are the same man. Don't know that—yet." Her eyes now gleamed with amusement.

There was a long pause.

The bitch had him. She might as well have pulled a gun. He was right in the heart of the enemy. He couldn't afford to have his cover ripped off. He needed time. This called for a strategic retreat or, better, yet, graceful surrender.

He looked at her body. It was nutty, in a way, to turn down a woman stacked like her, all tits and buttocks and a sweet full mouth. His body began to simmer.

She'd been watching like a hawk and picked

up the male instinct at work. She smiled, and without a word, as if she understood what would happen next, she started to unbutton her shirt. He watched as her deep breasts came into view, with the delightful pink nipples. Her skin was milk-white, and as the sun hit her breasts he felt the animal in him coming up strong. He stood still as she pulled off her boots and pulled down her riding pants.

She stood there, a real feast, her skin silky, gleaming in the sun, her tummy flat with its belly button, her solid buttocks a thing of beauty. Between her ripe thighs, her red pubic hair did a discreet but not complete job of covering her sex.

"Well," he said, swallowing, "nobody is gonna call me a sore loser." He stripped, grabbed the bedroll from the pinto, and moved Maude down upon it. He kissed her mouth, felt her hands sliding down his body, reaching for his bristling excitement. She's one hungry woman, he thought, and he went for her breasts, working on them with his lips and tongue, feeling her breath quickening. She slipped down on his body as if she had to see the towering excitement for herself, and she gazed then with sudden greed, opening her full lips as if trying to get him all at once. Her movements were expert and hungry, as she held him, working her mouth like a woman starved for love. He felt himself go massive with pleasure. Finally he pulled back, turned her, looked appreciatively at her firm, beautifully curved buttocks, slipped between them into the luscious groove.

He grasped her breasts and twisted his bigness in and out. She felt amazingly tight, and the sensation was pure pleasure, climbing, as he moved, to a pitch, never pausing, building momentum.

Her body shuddered as if she'd been hit by a bolt, but he never stopped, kept driving on and on, feeling the slow surge in him build until it became the agonized moment of pleasure. It started wild waves in her, and her hips went crazy with rhythm. He felt her pressing, as if she wanted to get her body into his. They stayed tight until he became aware of the gentle sun, the boulders around that gave them privacy, the flight of a hawk above. There was a great terrain out there, he realized, and just now it belonged to Terry Larrabee. And he had just had sex again with the woman who belonged to Terry Larrabee. This was like putting your head in a noose twice! That's what came from following that gun in his pants, he thought. It'd be damned smart now to get a gun that was in his holster, which meant get into his jeans pronto, if he hoped to keep his skin intact. He pulled away from her and quickly dressed.

Fargo scanned the Red Hills, a landscape to the south that rippled with steep timbered rising slopes. Far as his eye could see, there was nothing, no horseman or horse. The sun was on the descent, and a mellow glow poured over the sky. Maude, by this time, had to be back at the ranch; obviously, it would have been indiscreet to ride back together. He'd gone on to survey the Red Hills, but he thought of Maude. A handful of woman who just might get addicted to snuggling in the sagebrush with him, and that'd spoil his own plans. He didn't intend to be a patsy for her sex grievances against Terry; it might explode things faster than he could handle.

As the pinto jogged back toward the big corrals, he wondered how to handle her. Because she could rip his cover, she literally had him by the balls. He had to keep out of her way.

When he reached the main corral, he saw Matty lurching drunkenly toward a fine-looking mare, very spirited, held by two men. Fargo's eyes narrowed; he brought his pinto toward the fence, noticing Terry nearby, talking to a tall lean wrangler.

Fargo swung off the pinto and climbed the fence to watch. This setup held nothing but the promise of trouble, he thought—a drunk and a nervous mare.

Two handlers held the mare, and Matty skidded off its back twice as the skittish horse lurched.

"Hold the damned hoss," Matty yelled. "How in hell can I break her if I can't get on?" His voice was guttural drunk. He caught sight of Fargo, grinned, and waved. "Clancy! Good to see you here. Watch me tame this bitch hoss."

Concentrating, he got a foot over and held on. The horse quivered, trembled, and only the hard grip of the two men kept it from bolting.

"Let her go," Matty yelled.

At the yell, Terry turned sharply, as if fully aware for the first time of what was happening; with a black scowl, he came quickly to the fence. He doesn't like it, thought Fargo, and me neither.

The mare, released, neighed loudly, responded to the sudden dig of spurs with a jump, a violent bucking and kicking. Matty, his reflexes muddled by liquor, came down wrong and dug brutally at the flanks, cursing, waving his arms. The mare, frightened and hurt, bucked more viciously, went up, almost fell backward. Matty cursed, dug his spurs deeper. Blood dripped from the mare's mouth, and blood gleamed at the haunches. It went up, pawed at the sky, neighed piteously, and Matty roweled her viciously. The mare screamed in pain.

Fargo felt a blinding rage and climbed the fence, ready to tear Matty off the horse. Terry, too, was yelling at Matty. The mare went into wild circles, and the force threw Matty clear. The horse kicked wildly, missing his head by inches.

A cowboy threw a lasso at the mare and held it while Matty, sputtering curses, got up and started toward the horse. Terry, who had climbed the fence, met him and yelled. "You stupid, blundering moron. I told you not to bust any horses." He swung a roundhouse, his fist crashing into Matty's jaw, knocking him flat on his back and out. Terry looked down at him, wheeled, saw Fargo at the fence, then started for the house.

Right thing to do, Fargo thought, brother or not. Anyone who treated a horse like that should be shot. The man was drunk, but that didn't excuse it. A cowboy had to know he had no right to try and break a gut-twister with almost a quart of booze in him.

One of the handlers lifted Matty, and he came awake. He struggled to his feet, looked for Terry. He put his hand to his jaw and winced. Then he saw Fargo. He came out of the corral and stood alongside Fargo at the fence.

"Did you see that, Clancy? My own brother. Hitting me. Did you see that?"

Fargo said nothing.

Matty cursed. "I'm not taking it anymore. One day I'm going to pull a gun." He held his jaw, then grinned. "He's got the punch of a mule's kick," he said grimly. "But tell me, Clancy, what'd I do wrong?"

The brat needed a hard spanking, and more. "Why in hell did you get on that gut-twister?"

Fargo demanded. "Even sober you couldn't ride it."

Matty looked wounded. "Clancy, don't say that. I know I looked the fool. But I can break that knothead. Sober, she'd be a push." He rubbed his chin, muttered to himself. He was drunk enough to spill the intimate details of his life. "Trouble is, Clancy, I ain't been sober much lately." He moved closer to Fargo. "It's that damned woman of mine."

"What do you mean?"

"It's Abigail. She's driving me to drink."

Fargo almost smiled. It was hard to believe that a woman like Abigail would drive a man to anything more than plain lust.

"How's she doing that?"

Matty grimaced. "She don't respect me. She won't do the wifely thing."

"You been fooling around, Matty?"

He shrugged. "Uh, well. There's Ruby Carson. I did fool around there. But stopped. Abigail won't forget, won't forgive. She's a hard woman. Don't know what to do." He looked at Fargo. "You're a man of experience, Clancy. What ought I do?"

Fargo looked at the mare in the corral, its eyes still wild, its chest still heaving. "I wouldn't try to ride her like you did that mare. You're not breaking a horse. Women don't respond much to rough treatment. Try the soft ways."

Matty shook his head. "She's hardheaded. That thing with Ruby, she holds it against me. That's why I been hitting the bottle. And Terry's down on me. Always finding fault. Always. It's no wonder I'm drinking."

*   *   *

At the evening meal in the chuckhouse, Fargo sat at a table with four cowboys and ate a thick sirloin, mashed potatoes, black-eyed peas, and a chunk of chocolate cake. Like Terry said, the grub was good.

Fargo took note of the red-faced man, Johnson, at his side, and Hardy, opposite, a man with a hawklike face and flat blue eyes that looked shifty. The men talked about horses; then Hardy, whose gaze slipped sideways at Fargo, finally asked, "Where you from, Clancy?"

His tone was not friendly, and Fargo didn't like it. Didn't like the man who looked like he had a lot of dirty ideas.

"From a lot of places. I'm well-traveled."

Hardy tried a grin on a cord of a mouth, but it looked like a grimace of pain. "Thought you might be from Dakota Territory."

"Been there." He lifted his coffee. "How come you ask?"

Hardy scowled. "If you want the truth . . ."

"We always want that, Hardy." Fargo smiled. The men laughed.

Hardy bit his lip and didn't like it. He leaned forward. "I heard how you beat Bronco. You gotta be fast for that. And I figgered you oughta have a big rep, wherever you came from." He glanced at the others. "When the Dakota Kid came here, he had a rep. Word gets around when a man's fast. Now the Bronc beat the Kid, and you beat the Bronc."

"What follows?" Fargo asked.

"Somebody should have heard of you," Hardy said.

Fargo studied the man: what was he after? He didn't seem itching for a showdown, didn't seem the type. He could be a game rooster who bristled when another rooster got into the pit. The territory crawled with men ready to fight a big man to prove they were bigger, and if you kept taking offense, your life would be nothing but fights.

"Maybe I just got lucky with Bronco," he said.

Hardy's eyes glittered. "A man can have a lucky day. I just figgered that you shoulda had a big rep. You came outta nowhere and beat Bronco, who beat the Kid, who, they say, was the baddest and fastest." Hardy glanced at the other men as if wanting their backup, but their faces were wary.

Fargo stroked his chin, then said softly. "I just wonder what you make of all that?"

Hardy felt pressure, but didn't care to go over the line. "No offense, Clancy. It's just my idea of how a story can get a bit bent. Take the case of the Dakota Kid, who had this big rep, so everyone steered clear of him. Then he said the wrong thing to Bronco and, pow, he got mowed down. So the story about the Kid being the fastest was a bit bent. That's what I mean. All the time he just wasn't that good."

There was a long moment of silence. There's nowhere to take this thing, Fargo thought.

Then Johnson laughed. "If you're not careful, Hardy, you might get a bit bent."

The men laughed and Hardy flushed, glanced at Fargo, and seeing him more amused than angry, he blustered. "Nobody bends Hardy," he said, and stared insolently at the others. The men stopped laughing.

Fargo smiled. There's wasn't much to like in Hardy. The man didn't want a fracas, just wanted to know, maybe, what made Clancy Brown tick. If Hardy had an enemy, he'd probably hit the man from a hidden window. Smart to keep a sharp eye on him. The men would like to see Hardy get his knuckles rapped, but he didn't intend to play gunfighter just to relieve the boredom of cowboys. Terry was his target.

He stood, nodded to the men, noted Hardy's grin of satisfaction, then went out the door. A low sun smeared the sky orange-red. Fargo looked at it, took a deep breath, then lit a cheroot. In the corral two men were inspecting the foreleg of a filly. A rustle and footstep behind him: it was Hardy, his hawkface in phony embarrassment. "Say, Clancy, hope I didn't offend you. I'm dumber than a mule, sometimes, shooting off my mouth."

Fargo nodded. "No offense taken." The man's face was as dishonest as a three-dollar bill.

Just then the door of the big house opened and Terry came out, followed by Maude. She stopped at the doorway and spoke in harsh low tones; he ignored her and walked off. Before she went back in, she saw Fargo, stared for a long moment, then shut the door.

A great piece of woman, that Maude Larrabee," Hardy said, his hawkface wrapped in a leer. "Gives a man bad dreams." He turned toward the bunkhouses. Fargo moved toward the corral; Hardy had a way of making himself real unlovable.

Terry, deep in thought, was on his way to his horse, a big fine black, tied to the post. He glanced up, saw Fargo; it was hard to read his face, not one that leaked the feelings behind it.

"Any luck in the Red Hills, Clancy?"

"Not yet."

"Keep poking around. The men are there. They're sly. You'll find them." He turned to his horse, anxious to go, then stopped. "I saw you at

77

the corral when I slugged Matty. He's my brother, and I love him, but he won't measure up. Damned disgrace the way he handled that mare. Not like him. But he's hitting the bottle. I can't manage him much." Terry bit his lip.

Fargo looked hard into Terry's eyes. "I'd have done just what you did, slugged him for the way he treated that mare. I'm glad to hear he's not that kind of man."

The gray eyes were troubled. "I remember him as a curly-headed kid, full of loving ways. But he's gone bad." His jaw firmed. "I know he respects you, Clancy. I may not be able to handle him, but he could listen to you. Maybe you can straighten him out."

Fargo shook his head. "It's the drinking. That's the main thing."

Terry's mind was on something else. "He'll listen to you. I gotta go." He walked to his horse, a powerful black with beautiful white marking on nose and chest. He swung over easy, nudged it toward the gate, and looked caught up in deep thought. It was this, more than anything else, that made Fargo decide, on the spur of the moment, to tail him.

Whatever his destination, it sure weighed heavy in his mind.

He looked at the print of the black and locked it in his memory. Now he could let Terry take a long lead, and he would pick the print up whenever he wanted. He flipped his cheroot in a high arc, looked at the sky with its creeping fingers of dark. He swung over the pinto and started for the gate. Terry's track went to the trail, then toward a rising slope. He was not headed for Spoon River; it didn't take much to guess his destination was Ruby's place.

The dark hit fast and a sickle moon cast a dim light on the earth. It took another half-hour before Fargo picked up the lights gleaming from the windows of the big white house where Ruby lived. He tethered the pinto to a branch, where the grazing was good, and went forward, using trees and brush for cover. He stopped and listened: only the hoot of an owl, the rush of a marmot into the bush. He moved closer, slowly. A lonely cowboy tune strummed by a guitar floated out from one of the bunks thirty yards from the big white house. He could hear other voices from the bunkhouse, men playing cards. He moved low and softly to the lighted side of the big house, which must be the living room. If it were a bedroom, then his trip was a waste; he didn't care to peep into Terry's tricks with Ruby.

Voices came clearly from the window before he reached it. It was Ruby's, and it was irritated. "You just don't *want* to understand. I told you again and again. It's not going to be different."

Terry's voice. "But you're pushing hard, honey. I need time." There was a rustle of movement.

"Don't try that, Terry. It won't work anymore. Not anymore."

Silence.

"I'm telling you, Ruby, there's gonna be a war. The government will need horses, lots of them. And that'll be a big payday. I'll have your money then, all of it. Now listen, I'll give you an extra ten percent of your money. I'll write a note."

"When's this war gonna happen? Tell me that. I been hearing rumblings for two years about your war and the government's need for horses."

"It's coming. I'm telling ya. I talked with a big man from the East. He knows. The cavalry must be built up. That means horses."

Long silence.

"Sounds like the same old story. Listen, honey, I don't like to push you on money. It's the other thing I want."

Silence.

"You know, Terry, it's downright insulting the way you do. You get a lot of my money, and I'm ready to help you more, if you need it. And you got my love. I did think I had your love too."

"You do, dammit, Ruby."

"Then why don't you take action? Tell me, why? Are you ashamed of me, that I might bring disgrace to the Larrabee name? Is that it?"

Terry's voice had an edge of pleading. "None of that, honey. You know how I feel about you. But I can't turn Maude out just like that. The Larrabees stand for something in Spoon River. People will talk."

"Let 'em talk," she said harshly. "They talk anyway. And they're always saying rotten things. You gotta keep in mind, Terry, that if not for my money, your famous Larrabee name would be nuthin', your ranch woulda gone bankrupt. I saved it, and saved you. It's 'cause I care for you, honey. But it's going nowhere. I want to be Mrs. Terry Larrabee, the lady of the Bar-L."

Fargo, listening, almost whistled.

"And you're gonna be, Ruby, dammit. You just let me work it out with Maude in my own time. I don't want a scandal. Neither do you. Everything's got to look nice and proper. Then you'll come in. You'll be the lady of the Bar-L. Trust me, Ruby."

Long silence.

"All right, Terry. And we're wasting time. Oh, I've been craving you. Here, lemme at you, honey." Her voice went husky.

Fargo smiled. The bitch would be working on

the buttons of his jeans, something she had a talent for. He backed out, moved slowly, putting down his feet with feather lightness, and he had reached the middle of the field when a shot of light flared out from the bunkhouse as the door flung open. He froze, aware that, though the moon was dim, he was clearly visible. His skin tingled and his hand was ready for the gun. The cowboy who came out, however, just wanted to empty a basin of water. He threw a hurried glance up at the moon, then shut the door, and the light disappeared.

Fargo took a quick breath. If the man had looked right, hell would have broken loose. He bent low, moved quickly toward the big tree trunk, his first cover. Then he heard a raucous growl, a plunging through the bushes west of the bunk. A coyote in pursuit of a marmot maybe. A squeal, the scrabbling of claws, furious action in the bush. He dug for the tree trunk, lightning-fast, slipped quietly behind it as the light again shot out of the bunkhouse.

A cowboy with a gun was silhouetted against the light. "What the hell's going on?"

"A coyote hunting. C'mon back. I got a hot hand."

"It's something else, Barry, I can tell."

"You lummox, you don't even know which way the wind is blowing. It's a coyote, so c'mon back. Lose your money like a man."

The cowboy, however, followed his own instincts and took a few more steps, peering around suspiciously. He seemed fascinated by the shadows of the tree, edged toward it. Suddenly there came a wail of frustration from the throat of the coyote, which had lost its evening meal.

"Son of a bitch," the cowboy cursed. He picked

up a stone and flung it at the bushes, which brought a scuttling of claws, then silence. Satisfied he'd restored safety to the night, the man took a casual glance around, went through the doorway, and the light disappeared.

One of life's gentle moments, thought Fargo, who didn't care in the least to get involved with a cowboy innocently doing guard duty.

He moved low and fast and didn't feel easy till he reached his horse. The pinto's ears had long since picked up his approach, and his big, black eyes gleamed in the soft moonlight.

As the pinto loped toward the Larrabee ranch, Fargo chewed on what he had heard: Terry was in hock to Ruby. Small wonder the Larrabees hung around her like bees to honey. She had them by the short hairs.

The Larrabee women didn't know about the leverage Ruby's money gave her on the Larrabees. They put it all down to a love spell. It was why they threw a jealous fit, why they pulled their guns on him for vengeful sex.

If Terry meant what he said, Maude's time was running out. Terry, a low-down hustler, seemed to want Ruby's charms and Ruby's money, and Ruby wanted respectability and the power that came from being the mistress of the Bar-L.

Terry would not sacrifice the Bar-L for any woman, not he.

Poor Maude.

At the Bar-L, he ran into Luke talking to a hired hand. Luke nodded without smiling, his eyes curious. Luke had lost friendly feelings since he saw Fargo look at Julia. A jealous ox of a man, and it didn't help, Fargo thought, to be on the wrong side of a monster like him.

"Been to town?" Luke asked casually.

"Just scouting," Fargo said.

Luke nodded. "Find anything?"

"Nothing."

"Maybe you could look harder. We just lost a couple of good blacks from the east corral."

Fargo's lips tightened. He didn't like anyone talking to him like that, but he had chosen to play the part of a wrangler looking for work, and as a hired hand, he had no right to beef.

"I'll look tomorrow," he said.

Luke's gray eyes held on his steadily. "I know you can *tame* horses, Clancy. But your job here is to *find* them." Then he smiled, but it wasn't friendly. "I don't think your mind is on your job."

"Why say that?"

"Just a feeling I got, Clancy. Not crazy the way you look at the women here. 'Course, they're attractive women, and I understand men can't help looking. Just keep hard in mind who the women belong to."

"I keep it in mind, Luke," Fargo said seriously. Inwardly he found it funny: it was the women who didn't keep in mind who they belonged to.

He drifted back to his bunk, thinking that Luke was down on him and that could be dangerous.

In the middle of the night, he came awake, aware of someone outside the bunk. The door creaked, opened, and a lean figure bulked against the dim light of the moon. That would be Conway back from prowling the trail for Terry. Fargo watched him come in, look curiously at his prone figure, then strike a match to light the lamp. What did he find on the trail? What did he know?

Fargo lifted on one elbow. "You'll be Conway."

83

The man grunted. He was dragging his ass.

"Name's Clancy Brown. I'm sharing the bunk."

"I see that."

"Hope you don't feel crowded."

Conway peeled his shirt. "Bunk's for two."

"Reckon you're tired and want your shut-eye."

Conway stared at him. "Might as well get acquainted, since you're bunking here." He was a lean man, sharp nose, lantern chin, brown eyes.

"What's Luke got you working on, Brown?"

"Rustlers."

Conway grinned. "That'll keep you busy. They keep pickin' off the horses. Must watch us all the time. They know when and where to hit. There's a bottle on the floor, Brown. Help yourself."

"Mighty kind, but next time maybe." Conway smiled as he picked up the bottle, held it to his mouth, and took a long swill. "That's good liquor." He took another swill and grinned. "That takes the crease outta your britches." He smiled at Fargo again.

"I'm riding into the Red Hills tomorrow morning, see if I can smoke out a rustler."

"They're smart devils." Conway fell back on the cot with a sigh of fatigue, took another drink. "This stuff's good."

"Had a hard trip?"

"Hard tracking. I was looking for three of our men." He paused, lit a cheroot.

"Find them?"

"Found three graves. Didn't bother to dig them up. It was them, all right. Got picked off by one man. Dunno how he did it. Scarface Smitty was a fast gun, and he had two backup men. But they're dead, and he's not. He was kind enough to bury them. Then he had the nerve to head for

Spoon River." He shook his head, looked at the bottle. "Like the taste of this booze."

Conway took another pull, wiped his mouth, then looked into the distance. "He's got balls, this gunfighter, riding into town. But I lost his tracks there. As far as I can make out, he's gone east. Don't know what to tell Terry. He's not one for an unfinished story. When he learns Smitty and the others got bushwhacked, he's going to blister my ass, even though it has nothing to do with me." He grinned at Fargo. "That's the kind of man you're working for, Brown."

Fargo nodded. This son of a bitch was a real tracker; he had put the story together from looking at prints. But naturally, he lost the tracks in town and stopped looking. That was his mistake. If you stop tracking, you miss your quarry when he could be under your very nose. He, after all, was the quarry, and right in the same bunk as the tracker. It was the last place for Conway to look. Still, the setup was dangerous, and if Conway were to discover that the man who got Scarface was living in his own bunk, he'd have to act fast.

"Well, you've had a long day, Conway."

"Yup. Glad you're in here, Brown. They could have stuck me with a fat wit." He blew out the lamp and within minutes was snoring.

Fargo listened and smiled grimly. Tomorrow could be an interesting day.

6

After breakfast next morning he ambled toward the big corral where Terry and four men hung on the fence, watching two wranglers put a saddle on a skittish black horse. Terry's eyes had circles beneath them, and he looked tired and sullen. Must have had a bad night thinking about Ruby, Fargo thought as he smiled and put himself astride the fence to watch the action. But the real action he had in mind was different. Conway, who was finishing breakfast, would be out here soon, and from this spot he could get an earful, yet not be conspicuous.

Fargo lit a cheroot and watched the horse, clearly unhappy about the saddle they finally strapped on his back. After a time, Fargo mused, the horse wouldn't feel comfortable without it.

From the corner of his eye, he noted Conway approaching Terry. Dull-eyed only a moment ago, Terry saw Conway and snapped alive. "Damn you, it's time you got back. What's happening? Where's Scarface?"

Conway squirmed. "Dead."

Terry stared at him. "Scarface, dead?"

"Dead. The others, too," said Conway, his face grim.

Terry was jolted. He ran his hand through his

red hair, then his eyes screwed tight. "And Fargo? Dead, too?"

"No, not him."

Terry flinched, as if hit. "You mean Fargo bushwhacked the men."

"He didn't bushwhack them. Came up on foot."

"Are you sure? How do you know they're dead?"

"Saw their graves."

"Who buried them?"

"The man who shot them."

Terry thought about it and his face grew dark with anger. "Where's this man now? Where'd he go?"

"I tracked him to Spoon River."

"Spoon River! Then where?"

Conway shrugged. "Dunno. Lost his tracks in town. I think he went east."

Terry's face went redder. "You think, you think. Why don't you know? I'm not paying you to think. Find out. Dig up the graves. Make sure it's them. I want to be sure about everything. Then get into town and ask. Ask about all strangers passing through the last few days. Go to the saloon. He must have stopped there. Take four men. I want Fargo. Grab him, bring him here. Wait. I'll get a description. Wait here. And don't screw up, Conway. It's your hide if you do." He turned and strode toward the big house.

Gone to squeeze more facts out of Maude, Fargo thought as he drifted toward the pinto. What would Maude do? He flipped his cheroot into the air, swung over the horse. Would Terry get the hard truth from her? If he did, the Bar-L would become the Bar-Hell. But Maude might think of their fun times in the bushes; in that case, she might muddy the picture. And she did

87

hate Terry's visits to Ruby. Maybe he should hightail out of here, fast, but somehow he didn't feel like running. What of Abigail, still in the clutch of the Larrabees? A honey girl and she needed help; she was the one who got away. He sighed. Why did a man always crave the one who got away?

He moved the pinto into a lope. His job, as Luke put it, was to track rustlers in the Red Hills. The sun was climbing and hit sharply on the mountain range, making a clean silhouette of the peaks. Morning dew still sparkled on the grass, and the scent of June flowers came strongly up to meet him.

Later, high up in the hills, the ground dived back down into valleys and then swooped back into hills. He stopped at a shallow stream to water the pinto. On the other side of the stream, he checked the ground carefully, found the print, finally, of a lone rider who also had watered his horse. A fresh print. He tracked the prints; they went to a high slope thick with cottonwoods. He moved cautiously. A big-winged bird to the left circled a few times, then flew west. He slid off the pinto, tethered it, then moved quietly ahead on foot. The lure of food, leftovers of men, perhaps, might have attracted the bird. He avoided twig and stone, moved noiselessly. A shift of breeze brought the smell of frying meat, then the low murmur of voices. He moved slower, never stepping until he was sure it would be soundless. The voices came clearer, and he felt one of them was familiar. He'd heard it somewhere. Recently. He moved the brush lightly, to peer at the two men at the fire. Hardy! Hardy and a man with a short black beard, tough, strong. But Hardy, what in hell was he doing here?

They talked in low tones, but he could hear.

"Not a good idea, Amos, not a good idea at all, picking up those two blacks. So soon after the other haul. It was too quick. Luke's in a rage."

"Let him rage. Hasn't done him any good." Amos laughed, lifted a piece of meat to his mouth.

"We can't push too hard. There could be a mistake. And I'm sitting there, right in the middle of them."

"You can be too careful, Hardy. You got nuthin' to worry about."

"There's always something to worry about. They got a new man trying to nail us."

"Who's that?"

"Clancy Brown."

"Clancy Brown. Never heard of him."

"He's tough, dangerous. Don't know where he came from. I tried to find out. Dakota, I think. Let's slow up for a week, till the heat's off."

"You worry too much, Hardy. The Larrabees have more horses than they can feed. We're doing them a favor, lifting them. Let them share the wealth."

"I'm telling you, they got this Clancy Brown. He's tough."

"To hell with Clancy Brown," said Amos.

Fargo stood up and stepped forward. "I'm sorry to hear you say that Amos. I'm Clancy."

They turned, startled. Amos clawed for his gun and had it out when Fargo's bullet hit his right eye, leaving a great gaping red hole; he lurched back and dropped like a lead sack. He squirmed for a moment and then went still. Hardy, in shock, had put up his hands, but was staring with wide eyes at Amos.

Fargo shook his head. "Shouldn't have gone for his gun." He looked at Hardy. "What are you doing in the rustling business? Thought you had more sense."

Hardy's face was drained white. He cleared his throat. "Nobody's got good sense." He looked down at the dead Amos.

Fargo rubbed his chin; this whole business stunk. Now he was bogged down with Hardy, not a man he cared much for. Fargo had come to Bar-L to get the lowdown on Terry—now he was trapped in a vendetta with rustlers. It made for a muddle. As a stealer of horses, Hardy was a miserable specimen of a man. It was a duty to bring him in. Let the Larrabees do the dirty work, squeeze him for where and how the rustlers operated. They were smart devils, as Conway said, planting Hardy as their man right inside the Larrabee ranch.

He came at Hardy from behind, lifted his gun, and threw it. The man's face was crumpled, probably he saw a rope in his future. Now he understood why Hardy worked to get a line on Clancy Brown. Funny the way he had said, "the story about the Kid . . . was a bit bent."

He grinned. "You look a bit bent, Hardy."

The lips in the hawkface tightened. "I was just fooling around, Clancy. I apologized, remember? You gotta be one great tracker to have picked us up." His smile was oily. "I got the friendliest feelings toward you."

"You're real friendly, Hardy. And it's a pain in the tail to me, but I've got to take you in."

Hardy tried to smile, but it came out wrong. "You might not have to. Maybe we can strike a bargain."

"What bargain?"

"Turn me loose. And I'll tell you about the

gang. Where they're holed up. How they get rid of the horses."

The man was gutless, he'd sell his grandmother. Fargo thought of the men who had gone to the rope without betraying him, the inside man.

"Talk to Terry. Maybe he'll buy."

Hardy swallowed. "I don't care much about talking to him."

"Don't blame you." He looked toward the horses. "Yours is the big gray. Move."

Hardy suddenly showed his anger. "It's three hours to the Larrabee ranch. You may not make it."

He expects help, Fargo thought. "I don't have to take you. I can drop you here." He put his hand on the butt of his gun.

Hardy paled. "A man like you wouldn't kill a man in cold blood."

"Do it if I had to," Fargo growled. "Don't give me any trouble on the way."

As they rode west, Hardy, on the big gray, would steal a glance left to the high slopes, and after fifteen minutes of riding, Fargo picked up movement. Five men on big black horses were riding parallel, and from even that distance he heard a yelp as they spurred their horses to a gallop. Hardy's face was grim with satisfaction.

His lousy sidekicks! Fargo cursed. "Stay ahead of me," he warned, "or I'll put a bullet in your hide." He slapped Hardy's big gray hard on the haunch and put the pinto into a run. The rustlers were out to shake Hardy loose and nail him. Hardy, their inside man, would be the last man they'd want to lose.

Dammit, he'd come to the Bar-L to get clear with Terry, not to get bogged down with a gang of rustlers. But whether he wanted or not, he was caught in the crossfire.

Hardy, he noted, was dragging his horse in hope of slowing their getaway. He put a bullet past Hardy's right cheek. "Move," he barked. That put greased skids under him, and he lashed the horse, but it was a heavy-footed plug, and Fargo figured his pursuers would reach shooting distance in twenty minutes.

A mile away, he spotted a dilapidated cabin, its logs decayed with weather and time.

"Make for the cabin," he yelled.

Hardy seemed to like the idea, thinking, of course, that his sidekicks would eventually smoke Fargo out.

Once you were holed up, you had to worry about food and water, so you'd have to break out. Not a good idea, holing up, Fargo thought, but he could do nothing else; that plug of Hardy's would bring little but ruin.

They jumped from their horses when they reached the cabin and Fargo grabbed his Sharps rifle from its saddle holster. It was a miserable hut, with a wooden chair, a hay bed, a ragged blanket, and side and front windows. The wood was split and rotten. "Stay in that corner," he told Hardy.

He stared through the front window at the five men riding hell-for-leather. They didn't know he had a Sharps; they wanted to get close and shoot the hut to pieces.

He put the Sharps on the window and sighted one of the riders in a checked shirt. He squeezed the trigger gently, and the rider catapulted back as if he'd been shot out of a cannon. The other riders, startled, jumped from their horses and hit the ground, crawling for cover. They'd get together and talk strategy, he supposed.

He turned sharply, though actually he'd heard no sound. Hardy had managed to tiptoe behind him, with a log in hand raised to crash his skull. Too late to swing his rifle, Fargo's hand went up to grab Hardy's arm, twist it, forcing him to drop the log. Hardy, with a quick move, made a grab for Fargo's throat. Fargo dropped the rifle, grabbed Hardy's fingers, and bent them back, almost breaking them as he pulled them away. He looked into Hardy's eyes; they were yellow with dirty white and glittered with fear and rage, like a trapped animal fighting for its life. He sent Hardy hurtling across the floor. Hardy hit the wall, bounced up, and rushed back, his head down to butt Fargo's gut. The trailsman's great hands stopped him in his tracks, and he brought up his knee sharply. Hardy barreled back, fell on the chair, splitting it. Doggedly he got to his feet, set on keeping Fargo battling so his friends outside could get in close. He came at Fargo with clenched fists; Fargo faked, swung a right that crashed against his jaw, and he went down like a log and lay still.

Fargo grabbed his rifle, peered at the landscape through the window. Nothing. They had used the fighting time to position themselves. Out there were trees, rocks, gullies, and plenty of places to hide. He'd have to stay damned alert. He wondered if he should put Hardy on ice. Tie him. Hardy groaned and his eyes opened—malice and hate shone in them.

"Try something like that again and I'll shoot your brains out," Fargo growled.

Hardy gritted his teeth. "What the hell have I got to lose, Fargo? It's the rope if you bring me

93

in. I might like the quick way." He sneaked a look out the window. "But I got a couple of friends out there. I may not have to go."

"It's your choice," Fargo grunted. "You won't get another chance. Don't try anything." He turned and examined the landscape. Nothing. They were out there, and Hardy had done a good job by diverting him. He had no idea where they were.

The gully was big enough for three or four men, then there was that big rock. They might be anywhere. He shouldn't give them a target. He put down the rifle and pulled his Colt, it was quicker.

After a few minutes of sharp watch, he chewed his lip, vexed. Getting mixed up with this rustler operation was a disaster. He rode into the Larrabee ranch to clear the problem of Terry. Instead, he was nailed down in a rotten little hut, fighting to bring in Hardy, a two-bit con man, and trapped by four rustlers. He didn't bargain for this when he started for Spoon River. Fate was a bitch—if you took two steps from your trail, you could find yourself in quicksand.

Something scratched his instinct, and he stopped breathing to listen. Something was wrong. A sound, yet not a sound. Not where a sound should be. He didn't have a handle on it, not yet, but if he didn't get it shortly, there'd be hell to pay. He felt it. There, he heard it again, and his brain, working with frantic speed, shot the message clearly. He went up on his toes, moved light as a feather two feet from the side window.

Hardy, puzzled, frowned and watched curiously. Fargo put a finger on his lips, pointed his gun.

There was absolute silence.

Then the head appeared upside down at the top of the window, and a gun and a hand started down.

Fargo fired. A dark crimson hole bloomed suddenly in the middle of the forehead, and for a moment the head hung there, blue eyes wide open, but vacant. The head shook, then slipped down, and the body from the roof followed after.

Gunfire spat through the front window and splintered the wood of the back wall. Fargo crawled to the front window. Two men firing from the gully, a third from the rock.

They kept fast firing, which tore the walls of the hut. Fargo waited; it was cover fire, they were planning a move. At the pause, he peered out: two men running for their horses, the third, at the rock, kept Fargo pinned down. He stayed down and thought of the man who made it to the roof. Good strategy. During the fight, he'd circled around to the back, crawled forward, got on the roof, figured to fire through the window. Clever. It might have worked, but Fargo picked up the soft sound, even though the rustler walked in his socks.

Pause in the gunfire: two riders were heading away from the hut, going east! The third man was running to his horse, crouched low. Fargo fired, and the bullet spun him in a circle and he fell.

He grabbed Hardy, "C'mon" he yelled, and pulled him outside. The horses were grazing nearby. They swung over the saddles and Fargo hit the haunch of the gray to make him run, they galloped west.

It didn't take long for Fargo to pick up the rustlers. They had moved back, for some reason, to let him come out; they had a play in mind. He wondered what. Did they think they could out-run him? Well, they had a point, with the plug Hardy was riding. They wanted him out of the hut.

Now they were coming hard; he turned to see one rider in a green shirt raise his gun and fire, the bullet whistling over his head. Fargo squeezed off a shot, the man clawed his chest, fell forward, a deadweight on his horse. The last rider, in a short black hat, pulled his horse, aimed carefully. Fargo, in a zigzag, couldn't shoot sharp, and felt a cold wave, expecting his body would take the bullet. Instead, there was a muted cry from Hardy, hit on the side of his head; the bullet lifted part of his skull, leaving a bloody wound. He pitched off his horse and fell facedown.

Fargo jumped from the pinto, twisted to fire, but the rider had turned back, keeping under cover. Fargo watched until he disappeared over the slope. He walked to Hardy's body. Dead. Then he brought the big gray over, lifted the body, threw it over the saddle. He looked again toward the high slope. The man in the black hat had shot Hardy deliberately!

Now he understood why they had backed off from the cabin. To let them out and get a clear shot at Hardy!

Why? To keep his mouth shut, that was why. Hardy was not a man to take a hanging without talking. They wanted to get the stranger first but, failing that, took Hardy. Their hideout was still a secret; Hardy was never going to betray the gang.

It was almost sundown when he reached the Bar-L with Hardy. Luke, leaning against the cor-ral fence, was chewing tobacco and watching a man spinning a lariat. Two other men sat on the fence. All were jarred as they looked at the body slung over the gray.

"That looks like Hardy," one said.

"What happened here?" Luke's voice rumbled from his chest.

"One of your rustlers," Fargo said.

"What's that?"

Fargo swung off the pinto. "Hardy worked from inside. Part of the gang. I picked him up in the Red Hills, at a meeting with a man named Amos. Hardy wanted the gang to slow up. Amos thought the Larrabees had enough horses to share." Fargo couldn't help smiling.

Luke's eyes were screwed tight. "Then what happened?"

"I walked in. Amos drew. I shot him. Started to take Hardy back. We got bushwhacked by some men. They tried to get me. I knocked them down. The last man then shot Hardy."

Luke digested it slowly, then spit tobacco. "Why'd he shoot Hardy? Why not you?"

Fargo looked grim. "That's what I asked myself. It has to be this—to keep Hardy from talking. Hardy knew everything. And he would have talked."

Luke's eyes glittered as if fifty thoughts were spinning in his brain. Then he nodded. "I'll tell Terry. Get some grub."

As he walked to the chuckhouse, he grit his teeth. Luke had all the personality of an ox, besides looking like one. And he didn't trust Fargo, not an inch, not since he saw how Fargo had looked at Julia. Might be big as an ox, but he was sharp, probably trusted his instincts. Fargo grinned. Lucky his instincts didn't spell out clearly that it had been Fargo who put the spurs on his lovely Julia. Her plump breasts and smooth body flashed to his mind; dammit, on this ranch he kept feeling as horny as a sex-starved goat.

He glanced at the big house, its windows glowing in the flame of the setting sun. And as he looked, a window on the second story opened—it was Maude, staring boldly toward him. A look like that had to be some signal . . . but what? His flesh crawled. Jesus, what if Luke had seen this! He shot a glance at Luke: the big man was working through the pockets of the dead Hardy and hadn't seen a thing.

After dinner he went straight to his bunk and lay on the cot. His time at the Larrabee ranch was running out, he could sense it. Terry was yelling for a description from Maude of exactly what the man looked like; Conway, the human hound dog, was sniffing down at the saloon; Luke was bristling with suspicion, and Maude was grabbing sex from him whenever she could. What next? As if in answer to his question, he heard a scratching at the door and then a woman's voice, "Clancy Brown?"

His flesh crawled. He was ready to sink into the floor if it was Maude, crazy for sex, coming here, this time of the evening, when anyone could walk in, including Conway.

He came to his feet, moved like a cat to the window to peer out. Abigail, for God's sake. He opened the door.

She came in, cool as a cucumber, in a brown silk shirt and brown riding pants. Her blond hair gleamed in the lamplight. She glanced around the bunkhouse, wrinkled her nose. "Not too clean, is it?"

"Needs a woman's touch." He grinned. Then he frowned. "Have you gone nutty, Miss Abigail?"

She casually took the chair. "Why'd you say that?" Her blue eyes fixed on him, and he found himself gaping back at her, that saucy mouth, golden hair, beautiful body.

"Listen," he growled, "nothing I like better than to look at you. But not like this. Conway could come in. Or some cowpoke."

The saucy mouth twisted with amusement. "Don't let your imagination run riot, Fargo. I'm not here to philander."

He couldn't help smiling. "I'm not sure I'm relieved to hear that."

"Nothing wrong in visiting my friend Clancy Brown, who saved the life of my dearly beloved husband. I don't propose to spend the evening here."

His eyes flicked over her body appreciatively. "Doggone, we don't need the whole evening to do some rip-roaring damage."

Her pretty face did not look amused. "I suggest you control your animal excitement. I'm here for another purpose."

He leaned forward. "How can I help you, Abigail?"

For the moment, it seemed, she almost looked fond of him, then her face went solemn.

"Were you serious about your offer to help? You see, I want to go home. I live in the town of Fremont, thirty miles north. I can't stand my life here, can't stand Matty anymore. He's a drunk, he's vicious, and I can't bear to let him touch me."

He shook his head. He knew Matty was a miserable worm, but he didn't realize how bad it must be for a woman like Abigail to live with him.

"Why can't you just walk out?"

"Matty won't let me go. And Terry keeps trying to patch it up. Looks bad for the Larrabees—that sort of thing. Even Luke's down on Matty, but when it comes to the Larrabee name, they stick together."

"I believe it. What can I do?"

She smiled, and it was a beautiful sight to him. "I want to know if I can count on you when I'm ready to make a move. I'll need a friend and an escort. I'll pay you. Whatever you ask. I may make this move soon. Can I count on you?"

He nodded. "Count on me." He scratched his cheek. "But you should know that anything can happen. Someone might break my cover. I may have to run."

Her brow furrowed. "There's no reason to run. Is there?"

"I hope not. But I think Terry's coming down hard on Maude to tell what she knows, what Fargo looks like, the details."

She shook her head. "I heard nothing about it. And Maude didn't mention it."

He thought of Maude staring out the window, sending him some kind of signal. Then he thought of Conway, Terry's hound dog, who might pick up something in Spoon River that would lead him right back here.

"Listen, if I have to make a run for it, we can meet in a prearranged spot." He thought for a moment, then grinned. "Like the big oak where we met the first time. In that real friendly way."

She stood, her eyes glittering. "We never met in that 'friendly way,' as you put it. I warn you, Fargo, to expect nothing but money for your help, for your escort. It's a business proposition." Her lovely mouth was firm and she looked no-nonsense. But that shape, those breasts and hips made his blood sing. He sighed instead. She was giving nothing but money. Money. He wouldn't take a dime from her and he'd give her all the help he could. She was all pure honey.

She went to the door and turned. "Thank you, Fargo. I think I'll sleep better tonight."

7

As for Fargo, he himself slept fitfully that night, and once, when his eyes opened, he glanced at Conway's bed—empty. His eyes closed, and he dreamed—this time that he was lying under a tree when Abigail, in tight britches, appeared with a gun. She kicked him awake, as she had before, and then, to his delight, she started to peel, holding the gun as if to force him into sex. He waited until she stripped bare, then grabbed the gun, pitched it away. "This is for fun," he said, and reached for her. But the beautiful body envisioned turned into air, and all he had left was emptiness. She faded away in his arms. He groaned and opened his eyes. It was morning.

He felt like a lion in heat and gritted his teeth. At the chuckhouse, he ate five hotcakes and ham, three buttered biscuits, and coffee. He came into the morning light, ready to roar aloud. He glanced at the big house. There was Maude again at the window, her great breasts almost jumping out of her shirt. His own thing jumped, and he clenched his hands and strode toward the stable. Three minutes later, he rode the pinto east, slowly; ten minutes later, she was riding, too, not far, but parallel. His groin ached with lust. The thought of Maude and her carnivorous ways put him into a burn.

The Larrabee land stretched for miles, and he pointed to the great boulders; they'd been there before. She rode smart, never directly behind, but off to the west. He studied the landscape—nobody but her. He slid off the pinto, took the bedroll, threw it alongside the big boulder, and waited. The sun hit his groin—there was hell to pay down there. He cursed gently; it was times like these for which women like Maude were invented.

He heard her horse before she appeared, and he was ready. He could hardly hold back the bulge in his britches.

She came in on her gelding, her blue shirt open to reveal her white flesh. She looked down, noted his hefty bulge. A small smile twisted her lips. "The cowpoke seems ready," she said coyly.

He watched her move, and simmered. "Hurry up," he growled suddenly.

A great smile flashed over her face. "Ah, the great lover is hungry."

Bet your sweet ass, he thought, and he helped her vigorously off the horse, opening the buttons of her shirt. Her white breasts leaped out, and he took one in his mouth, loving it with his tongue. He pulled at her boots and breeches, and soon her naked body looked shocking white against the gray boulder. He looked down at her red pubic hair, its pink crease, and in a gust of passion dropped to his knees. His hands grabbed her buttocks, and he pressed to her, giving her slow lingering touches with his mouth. Her body tightened under his caresses; his hands fondled the silk of her buttocks. Bursting with passion, he came up and opened the buttons of his britches, bringing out his bristling excitement.

She stared in wonder, caressed it, lifted her

lips, pulled against him. He felt driven to thrust at her. Finally, he brought her down to the bedroll; his hard body went over her smooth, soft curves. He probed between her thighs, slipped into the velvet warmth, pierced deep. He looked down: her eyes burned with desire, her red hair spread behind her like a red halo, but her passion was not angelic. She brought up her hips and he felt her body engulf him. He felt full, rigid, bursting with potency. He started to move, built up a rhythm, and before long, he was pummeling her with his maleness, while she gasped, whimpered, moaned. He went on and on until finally he felt himself escalate to a shattering rush of pleasure. She groaned with anguish at her sensations.

Later, Maude put on her clothing slowly, as if she were still in something of a trance. "Where in hell did you learn to make love like that?" she asked, her voice still quivering.

He slipped into his jeans, gave her a wicked grin. "Making good love is a gift from the gods, Maude."

"The gods overlooked Terry when they passed that out," she muttered. She fluffed her hair. "Oh, Terry's a man, no doubt about that. He's just a self-centered bull."

Fully dressed and the rage of desire now calmed, Fargo tried to focus on other urgent matters.

"Why do you trick Terry?" he asked.

She shot him a hard look. "Are you complaining?"

"No, just curious."

"Curious! I told you, he runs to Ruby like a lapdog to its mistress. He's a low-down skunk, and you're the one big reason I can take it." She flashed him a brilliant smile. "I've got the better man."

He leaned back against the boulder. "Anything unusual happen yesterday morning? Tell me, Maude."

She frowned. "Yesterday morning. Oh." She nodded suddenly as memories flowed over her. "Terry stormed in. Little man playing master of the house. 'Tell me,' he bellows, 'everything you know about Fargo. Everything, you bitch!' I gave him the cold eye. 'Tell me everything you know about Ruby,' I said. That snapped his head back. So he growled, 'Listen, damn you, I want a description of the man. What he looks like. His looks, his clothes, his horse.'

" 'Why do you want that, Mr. Larrabee?' I said. ' 'Cause I'm gonna crush him like a flea, that's why. Now tell me.' And he grabbed my arm. I looked at him cold as ice, and he dropped my arm. You see, Fargo, men roar like lions when they're with other men, but when they're with women, they roar like pussycats, if you got something on them. I could tell he wouldn't go away until I gave him something. So I said, 'Fargo is not tall, light-skinned, brown eyes, wears a green shirt, and rides a black horse.' Then Terry groans, 'Why did you do this to me, Maude?' His voice is full of pain. 'Why did you do it to *me*?' I says. He gave me a look of poison and stormed out. Heard him yelling, but it was all empty sound."

Fargo grinned, she was a regular whip. "That was a wild description of me."

"You're my big honey bear, Fargo. Don't want to lose you."

In a way he hated losing her too, but he could hear the howling of the wolves and his instinct told him that if he hoped to keep his skin intact, he'd better make a quick run for it, and pretty damned soon.

She was dressed now, with her tight shirt and riding pants, looking like a sexy doll. It was hard to believe that only minutes ago he had been deep into the lush flesh between those fine thighs. He felt a new throb in his groin and wondered if he should hit her one more time, for the road. It would be like tempting fate, and so he quickly passed up the idea.

Then he wondered if he should tell her that Ruby had a money hold on Terry. But that might open a new can of worms. She'd probably hit Terry with it. He'd want to know how she learned it. He'd bear down hard, and then she'd tell. If they ever bottled him on the ranch, it would be bad. And how would it help her to know? If Terry planned to drum her off the ranch, he'd do it, whatever she knew.

No! Telling her about Ruby would put a stick of dynamite in her hand that might just blow his cover.

"What are you thinking about, Fargo?"

He grinned. "I'm thinking that if I have to run for it, it's gonna be miserable leaving you behind."

"Don't run. You're safe here. The ladies like you. And that's protection."

He grunted; that was why he was sitting on dynamite.

"Time to go." He stood up.

They went back by different trails, she going south, the longer way around. When he reached his own bunkhouse, the sun was at the zenith; its heat, and the heat of the day's activities, made his eyes feel heavy. He decided to stop at the bunkhouse and stretch out, let his energy renew itself.

To his surprise, Conway was also in his cot sleeping, obviously resting from a gigantic output of effort. The squawk of the door hinges had awakened him, however, and his eyes flashed open, gleaming curiously at the sight of Fargo.

Fargo stayed casual. "Sorry, Conway. Go back to sleep, I'll move soft."

"No, it's all right," Conway said, pulling up on the pillow, but staying for comfort under his blanket. Then he grinned. "Hey, Clancy, that was a clever piece of work you did with Hardy. Heard about it." He shook his head. "That damned Hardy, slick as a snake. Nobody had a line on him. I always thought him a shady guy, but never figgered he was in the gang." He smiled sardonically. "Can't go by appearances."

"Guess not." Fargo's alarm system had gone off because of something about Conway, something different. But the alarm may have been false. Conway had heard of his exploit with Hardy, which could explain a change in attitude.

"What made you suspect him, Clancy?"

A bottle of whiskey was perched between the cots—Conway sure liked his booze. "Didn't suspect him. Didn't care for him. I rode out to the Red Hills, picked up a track, stayed with it. I lucked into a rustler confab. Hardy was there."

Conway grinned, lifted his head on the pillow, but still stayed under the blankets. Something scratched at Fargo, and he knew the feeling. He felt uneasy; his mind raced over possibilities.

"You're one hell of a tracker, Clancy. They sent me out there, but I never landed a fish."

"They got you tracking now, I heard."

"Yeah. Man called Fargo. 'Not tall, brown eyes,

green shirt, black horse.' One helluva steer. Nobody like that and everybody like that." His grin was devilish. "The only stranger who came into town that day was you. And you don't fit the description. But you are a fast gun. You beat Bronco." He grinned. "The man who knocked off Scarface was fast too." He shook his head and complained. "You can't trust anyone anymore. Here you are, right in my own bunk, Fargo, and I'm looking for you miles away." A gun pointed at Fargo from under the blankets.

Dammit, his alarm system never failed.

"Don't make a wrong move, Fargo, or I'll blow you to pieces."

"You're plenty sharp, Conway, gotta hand it to you. How'd you get onto it?"

That touched Conway's pride. He grunted. "Fast shooting, you blowing into the saloon at the right time. And your little talk with Denny about Terry. That put you hard in mind as a suspect. Then I knew the print of your pinto, and your boot. Saw the print outside this damned bunkhouse. It all fit."

"And you told Terry, I suppose."

Conway nodded.

"How come he hasn't tried to pick me up?"

"They didn't expect you'd come here midday. But just in case, I'm here. They're waiting down at the corral. All the Larrabees. I don't know what you've done, but I see a gang of men thirsting hard for a string-up. It's a pity, Fargo, 'cause, as I said, I kinda like you."

Fargo, who had been waiting for Conway to lift himself out of bed, watched as he put his elbow on the pillow.

"I could use a last drink," Fargo said.

"Why not?" Conway answered. He was feeling confident.

Fargo lifted the whiskey bottle to his lips. But, with a lightning twist of his wrist, he threw the bottle straight at Conway's eyes. Instinctively Conway flung his gun hand up to protect himself.

Fargo leaped, caught the hand, twisted it hard, crushing, hearing the crack of the bones as the gun dropped. Fargo swung hard at Conway's jaw, and he went solidly out.

"I kinda liked you, too," Fargo said.

8

He pulled Conway's belt off, tied his wrists, and dumped him on the bed. He grabbed his own few personal things and went out the door in a hurry. The pinto picked up his tension. Its ears shot up, its black eyes glowed as if he knew there'd be good running ahead. Fargo swung over the saddle, starting north with a vague idea of hitting the high boulder country, a good place for defense in case the Larrabees came at him hard.

He heard a yell—three riders, one pointing, sent by Terry, no doubt, to check on Conway. They were Terry's men—floaters, used for muscle or gun work, like Scarface. They rode big, deep-chested blacks, which shot out at the spur.

Fargo cursed. Terry, that crafty bastard, didn't leave anything to chance. If a slipup did happen with Conway, he'd have these wolves on the trail with fangs out. What were their orders: to capture or kill? He'd learn pretty damned quick when the pinto pulled away. With his great heart and magnificent legs, he'd pull away. Now, racing on level ground, it began to happen. He kept a sharp eye on his pursuers, easily done, given the marvelous even rhythm of the pinto's run.

Now the biggest man in the group, one wearing a checked shirt, seemed disappointed at the way his horse lost pace, so he reached for his gun.

Fargo knew then the orders Terry had given: "If you can't get him, kill him." He fired, and Fargo felt a burn on the edge of his left arm. Son of a bitch! His own gun barked and the big man grabbed at his throat, his head flung back; he danced crazily in the saddle and then toppled off. A second rider pulled his gun, and Fargo snapped off another shot that hit the man's shooting arm. Though jarred, he managed to stay in the saddle and pull the horse to a stop. The third rider, aware then he was pursuing a man who, when he wanted, could hit your shooting arm even from a fast-running horse, decided not to try his luck. He pulled up, shouted at the other man, let Fargo move out of gun range, but followed at a slow gait.

This mangy dog, Fargo thought, would stick with him while the other reported back to Terry. Before long, the Larrabees and their henchmen would be sweating his trail. He took a deep breath. Well, it wouldn't be the first time he'd been hare to the hounds. He glanced at his arm—a slight leakage of blood, a flesh wound. He'd have to bind it soon to avoid blood loss, in case the run ahead would be very long. Riding never helped any wound like this.

He eased the pinto into an easy lope, working toward higher ground and a cluster of crags that towered in the afternoon sun. The sky was hard blue, and he had a good piece of time before sundown. He'd have to work out a plan, and damned quick, because his position was less than good—in fact, it was lousy. He was surrounded by mountain ranges and didn't know of any pass. He seemed to be in a bowl, with no apparent opening; the mountains loomed up like an impassable trap. Suddenly he felt what an animal must feel when it discovered that escape was blocked and that, in the end, it would have to be cornered. He felt a spurt of anger. He never liked being cornered and didn't intend that to happen.

He turned and scrutinized the man who was tailing him, still staying out of range. A buckskin shirt, short-brimmed stetson, built lean and tight. He rode a deep-chested, long horse. Who was he? He had to be mangy if he gunned for a man like Terry. He rode easy, looked good in the saddle, and had about him the look of a hound dog. Not easy to shake, but perhaps he could still be pushed back. He pulled the Sharps from its saddle holster, sighted, and squeezed the trigger. Dust in front of the horse jumped, and the horse went up as the rider pulled the reins. Jolted to realize that Fargo could have picked him off, the rider turned the horse and raced back, out of range, then stopped. After a few minutes, he moved slowly forward.

More of a bulldog than a hound dog, Fargo thought, and he scowled. In a hunt, the way you survived was to destroy your hunters. All he had done was to wing them and warn them. An act of charity could prove fatal. Still, this rider had not pulled his gun; he must be following orders.

Fargo eased the pace of the pinto and studied the terrain. He had no clear plan yet, and if, as he expected, the Larrabees and their henchmen came stomping up, he'd better have a good position. Not only that, he needed to find a pass. There was a slope to the left, scattered with boulders; after a hundred yards, it began to climb steeply. He moved the pinto up and, after the long climb, stopped to look down. His pursuer was a small figure beside his horse, drinking from a canteen. Fargo realized that he, too, was thirsty and hungry. He pulled his canteen and, as he drank, studied the position. Not bad, but vulnerable on his flanks; still, he had a commanding view, and with his Sharps rifle, provided he was not caught off guard, he could keep them at a safe distance.

He looked at his wound: a piece of flesh nicked on the outer part of his arm. Lower, it would have hit the bone. He pulled out cloth strips he kept in his saddlebag and wound one tightly around the wound, certain it would, in time, stem the blood leakage.

It was a good idea, he thought, to keep a sharp eye for fresh game; you had to eat good to stay strong. He decided to keep moving up for a still-better position, and after a time, he felt the heat lessen. The sun had slid down and night wasn't far off. A fluff of white skittered along the periphery of his eye and his gun barked. A plump rabbit—that meant fresh meat at least for two days. He skinned the rabbit, put the meat in a leather pouch, then found a spot where boulders and bushes gave good camouflage. He had a commanding view and could still make out in the gathering dusk the tiny figure of his stubborn tracker.

Time for fire and a piece of juicy fried rabbit. It didn't take too long for the meat to sizzle in his fry pan and the coffeepot to boil. He cut strips of the tender meat, chewed it, washed it down with warm, bracing coffee. He ate a hefty portion of the meat, felt its nourishment flow through his body. The coffee gave a lift to his spirits, and he gazed into the glow of the fire, feeling a curious surge of pleasure. It was a rare, special feeling, and he wondered why it happened.

He was alone, except for the best companion,

his great Ovaro. A quarter moon in the sky shone silver-bright on a great spread of dark blue. A million diamonds glittered above him. And down on earth, the great mountain, massive and mysterious, surrounded him. So what caused this strange feeling of pleasure? He was a man alone, and all around him, the mystery of nature, as man had always been since the beginning. And beyond the fire, in the dark, lurked danger, the threat to life. But inside was the belief in himself, in his power to match the evil out to destroy him. An age-old scene—man against his enemy, and the fight, though it had the smell of death, also had in it the excitement and joy of battle.

He sipped from his tin cup and smiled. His thoughts were wild, and probably came only from the good coffee and fresh piece of meat.

He took time, after this, to run a fast curry over the pinto. Then he laid out his bedroll, put his gun near his hand, and once more looked up at the glittering stars.

Sleep hit him like a hammer. But he dreamed of Abigail with the blond hair, the saucy mouth, and those blue eyes, which, in his dream, seemed gloomy.

"I told you, Fargo, this place is a death trap. Why didn't you listen? If you go down, how will I ever get away from the Larrabees?"

He woke with an ache of guilt; somehow, one way or another, he must find a way to get back to her and help. Daylight was creeping in. He felt uneasy and looked over the broad edge of the rock, back toward his tracker. A cloud of dust was swirling, coming straight for him—Terry and his henchmen racing for a showdown.

He let out a string of curses. No doubt about it; Terry, that bastard, was after his hide and wouldn't spare horse or man until he got it. That posse, to make this spot so quickly, must have been riding long before sunup. So there was the enemy—a posse and three Larrabees—and all wanted him dead. But he never had a taste for cooperating with men who wanted him dead. Nearby was a wedged crag, right for positioning his Sharps rifle.

They had stopped, gathered around the front rider, looking at tracks and up the steep climb. The man in buckskin, the Larrabee's tracker, was pointing toward his boulder, a good eye. Though a good distance off, Fargo could still recognize the huge frame of Luke, the contours of Terry, and that hound-dog Conway.

No hurry, he was out of rifle range. He packed his gear, moved the pinto still farther back safely behind a rock, then positioned himself at the wedged crag. Excited at a sight of him, several men fired. He shrugged; at this distance, it was idiotic. Looked like Terry was in a hurry to have him dead; there'd be no question then, and his family honor and male pride would be satisfied. All he wanted was Fargo dead and in an un-marked grave. A dozen against one, but he had position and the weapon. War, he thought, comes down to the right position and the right weapon.

They came, bunched up, to the beginning of the slope, paused for a talk on strategy. More pointing, and, of course, the realization that they could hit him only frontally, that they had to climb the slope and work to get behind cover, but that, from his position, he could pour down firepower. They may have realized it didn't look good, but they didn't realize how bad. Fargo smiled grimly. His rifle was a long-range killer, and though they didn't dream it, he could hit them even now. He had no desire for a massacre, but he should let them know he was trouble, deep trouble.

He sighted on the man talking, the one who did the pointing; he had leadership, a fatal quality. Fargo squeezed the trigger gently and the man staggered, then fell like a rag in a heap. The other men looked around wildly, wondering where the shot came from, disbelieving that Fargo could have done it from such a distance. He'd let them know, however, and sighted next on a big man under a big stetson. A squeeze of the trigger and then that one grabbed his chest as if trying to dig something out, and then collapsed.

That did it; they started to run for cover, well aware of where the shooting came from. He picked off one more, a man in a red-checked shirt racing for a boulder; the bullet catapulted him forward and he hit the ground smash on his face.

Everything was clear now, but for the horses. Terry's men would stay nailed down, at least for a time; they had to to take care of the fallen men.

While they lurked behind cover, Fargo slipped back to where he tethered the pinto, mounted, and started to ride. They still had the odds, but it wasn't overwhelming. And he had given himself some leeway.

He reached the crest of the slope in a matter of moments, then swung quickly to the other side. From here, the terrain looked smooth and flowed into a valley, a landscape of trees and bushes. The pinto went down, easy, surefooted, and as the ground leveled out more, Fargo spurred him to a faster pace. Terry was bogged down with wounded men; it would take a good bite of time before he learned if he still faced that deadly rifle straight on.

Yes, Fargo thought, fear would pin them down, but they'd come, after that, hellbent for revenge. He smiled: hot blood, poor judgment. In his mind, he could see them all bunched up, racing hard on his trail. A man like Terry, he was sure, would not be happy with just bloodletting; he'd want a hanging, or even worse. Only violence would appeal to his lust for revenge.

He rode two more hours, then stopped for the pinto to drink. He chewed a few strips of meat and thought coffee would taste good, but decided against a fire, not now; he'd wait for a stronger position. He had been studying for some time the northwest side of the mountain, a gap between towering crags, wondering if it might offer a pass. He liked the direction—it let him move in a great circle. Abigail was still unfinished business. How to help her was a riddle though, just now, he needed more to concentrate on helping himself.

After riding another hour, he came to a steep column of stone, climbed it, and stared southeast. It took a sharp lookout to locate them, a tiny swirl of dust—they were two hours behind.

He grinned, it all had worked out nicely. He had a big lead, and he now could see the two towering crags with what looked like a gap between them. It might be a pass or a dead-end. He had to chance it, though he might end up trapped like a rat.

He could use water for the pinto, it had been working hard. Fargo let his eye rove: there—a stream tumbling from a slope, back to the west. It ran past a cave burrowed into the mountain, a place where men through the ages probably protected themselves against weather. He'd get the pinto its water, refill his canteen, and rest before he started for the towers. It took half an hour to reach the stream. He swung off the pinto, led it to the water, filled his canteen. Then he walked to the mouth of the cave. It was dark, and it took time for his eyes to adjust to the dim light. But his ears needed no adjustment.

"We've been waiting, Fargo. What took you so long?"

The gun on him was held by the man in the buckskin shirt, the lone tracker who had stuck with him when the others dropped. Behind him two men were grinning.

"Knew you'd come to this stream, eventually," the tracker said. "Now, your gun—hold it by the butt with your fingers, then drop it. Don't even breathe or you're dead."

They had him.

"Nice work, Hawkeye," said a man with a pock-marked face. Then a lean, stubble-bearded man came out grinning. "Yeah, Hawkeye, you called the shot."

"Get his gun, Butch," Hawkeye said. The pock-marked man picked up the Colt, looked at it curiously. "This son of a bitch can shoot."

"Done his last shoot," Hawkeye said, his face hard. "Now he's ready to hang."

"Should we tie him?"

"What for? He makes a move, shoot him in the balls. But don't kill him. Strict orders. Terry wants a hanging."

Butch stared at Fargo, then growled. "Wish he'd give us the excuse to shoot his balls off. Think of what he did to our men."

Hawkeye scowled. "We follow orders, Butch, understand? Terry will rip our hides otherwise." He turned to the stubble-bearded man. "You, too, Polecat, keep it in mind. No vendetta. We all want to fry this guy, but let Terry do the honors. He's got a lot on his mind about Fargo."

"So what do we do?" Polecat asked.

"We wait. They'll know where we are, and they'll make it long before sundown."

"Goddamn, I'm hungry," Polecat said.

Hawkeye scowled. "You eat like a hyena and never put on a pound. How come?"

Polecat shrugged. "Sort of nervous."

Fargo's lips pressed tightly as he thought of something. "Got some rabbit in the pouch. You're welcome to it," he said.

Hawkeye grinned. "Mighty nice of you, Fargo. Seeing as you ain't got much of a future, you won't need the nourishment. Make a fire, Polecat."

"I'll get it for you," said Fargo.

Hawkeye stared hard. "Just stay put, mister. You don't move an inch unless we tell you. Get it? Butch, you go for the meat."

Rummaging in Fargo's saddlebags, Butch brought out meat, beans, and coffee.

Hawkeye laughed, "Fargo does all right. And not only with food."

"What do you mean?" asked Butch as he opened the can of beans, put it into the saucepan.

Hawkeye smirked. "I think he tripped one of the Larrabee ladies."

The men stared at him. "Why do you think that?" Butch asked.

"It's a whisper. Conway picked it up. Heard the Larrabees beefing about it once, before they sent him out to find Scarface." Hawkeye turned to Fargo. "That right, mister? That you been playing ball with one of those beautiful Larrabee ladies?"

Fargo's face stayed carved in stone.

Hawkeye grinned. "He's a gentleman, won't talk."

"I'll make him talk," Polecat said as he lit the fire. "Make him sing like a bird."

Hawkeye yawned. "I doubt it. And don't try any funny stuff. This guy's dynamite. You know that he knocked off Bronco in a shootout."

"He did!" Polecat's eyes widened.

Butch shrugged. "He's like all the rest. Get his gun and he's a pussycat. Look at him—we pulled his claws, right?"

The men grinned. The meat was beginning to sizzle and the beans and coffee were simmering.

"You're a good tracker," Fargo said to Hawkeye.

Hawkeye studied him. "I can follow a trail," he said modestly.

"You hung on to me real good," Fargo said, cursing himself for not knocking him out when he had the chance. You should kill your hunters when it's the only way to survive. He didn't have much time before the Larrabees would come galloping up. And they'd make a Roman holiday out of him; a sadistic bastard like Terry would want payment in full.

He put on a casual front. "You know, Hawkeye, I could have picked you off."

Hawkeye laughed. "Yes, that was one real idiot move. You had me and passed it up. Mistakes like that put a man at the end of a rope."

They were eating, each with a plate of meat and beans and a tin cup of coffee.

He wanted them eating, that was why he had suggested the rabbit. He watched them, seemingly at ease, but his pulse hammered. He didn't have much time. Once the Larrabees got here, he had the chance of a snowball in hell. He wanted them eating because it tied up their hands.

He studied the setup, to figure out each move; everything had to mesh or he was gone. He had a two-bladed knife in his boot. Hawkeye was the smartest and fastest; Butch could be fast, he'd have to hit him second; and if he himself was still alive, he'd go for Polecat then. But everything had to fall in place, the timing and the moves.

"Hawkeye," he said.

"Yeah?"

"You know, Hawkeye, since I didn't pick you off when I had the chance, I think that rates, at least, a cup of coffee."

Hawkeye stopped eating, stared at him shrewdly, saw no harm in it, "I suppose so. The condemned man deserves a cup of coffee." He was pleased by his wit. "Give him a cup, Polecat."

Polecat growled, he didn't like to stop eating to service a lousy cowboy who'd be hanging within the hour. He poured hot steaming coffee into an empty tin cup, brought it to Fargo, who was sitting with his knees up. He turned and started to his place at the fire.

Fargo's moves were lightning-quick. He slipped the knife from his boot, held the coffee steady in one hand, and threw the thin-bladed knife with the other. It hit Hawkeye's chest, slid in up to the hilt; his body quivered, his eyes rolled wildly. The others didn't yet know what happened. Fargo flung the hot coffee at Butch's eyes, blinding him; he screamed, pawed at his eyes; Fargo grabbed the saucepan of beans, smashed it against the back of Polecat's head, hurtling him forward to hit the ground. A grab at Butch's gun, a bullet into the back of Polecat's head, and one into Butch's heart. Blood, brains, and gristle seemed scattered everywhere.

It all happened in four seconds.

Hawkeye, still alive, was trying to pull the knife from his chest; his eyes were on Fargo, the look in them unreadable. His lips opened.

"Shoulda shot you dead . . . at the beginning . . . you bastard," he said. And died.

Fargo grabbed the meat from the plates, no point wasting it. He'd need it later, he thought, and even drank the unfinished coffee. He packed his saddlebag, looked at the three men, sprawled in death, then at the Larrabee bunch, climbing slowly toward him. His teeth gritted and he climbed onto the pinto and started riding.

It was almost noon, and the sun hit down harshly. He studied the land ahead, where it became gulleys and ridges, good for defense. By now the Larrabees knew that Hawkeye's trick of heading him off hadn't worked. They were still coming. Probably they felt they had him trapped anyway, with no pass through the mountain. He put the pinto into hard climbing and, after a sweaty two hours, found a good crag for defense. He swung off the pinto, chewed the meat strips, drank from his canteen. He could still see them climbing, they weren't sparing the horses. Terry kept pressure on his men.

He looked northwest at the gorgelike gap and what he hoped might be a pass. It would take four hours more to reach it, about sundown. If it were a dead-end, he'd be bottled up. Meanwhile he had an immediate crisis. They were coming fast, all bunched up. They could use a cool-down. His arm felt wet, bloody; dammit, the wound had kept leaking. But he couldn't worry about that now.

He pulled the rifle and got a good position behind the crag. He could sight them, but still he waited. The lead rider, Conway, held up his hand. They stopped. Two men slipped off their horses, came forward in a crouch, guns drawn, running cover to cover, exposed for short bursts of time.

A man in blue denim ran from behind a tree, bent low, searching for his target. He almost reached his next cover when Fargo's bullet hit him; he spun, grabbed at his shoulder, then fell stiffly. His sidekick, also in the open, scrambled for a rock, but Fargo's next bullet jerked him violently and he fell like a log. The men on horses scrambled madly for cover behind trees and rocks.

Fargo didn't waste a moment but raced to his pinto, jammed the rifle into its holster, climbed up, and started a run.

Now, with two more wounded, and one to care for them, the odds looked better.

He spurred the pinto, determined to get more space, just in case anyone still felt like coming on hard.

Four men did: Conway and the three Larrabees.

Now on level ground, he gave the pinto its head and stretched out full stride, it pulled away slowly and steadily from the trackers. When the sky went pink and the sun sunk lower, he eased the Ovaro into a lope. As he neared the mountain gap, the ground grew rockier. It would be impossible to tell if there was a pass until he got much, much closer. He needed that pass real bad. His arm felt wetter from the blood seepage. By his calculations, he had only twenty minutes left; in that time the sun would be down and dark would shroud the mountain.

He shot a glance behind him at the four bloodhounds, still riding steady. Did they know, he wondered, if he were blocked off, if he had trapped himself? He felt a rush of weariness, he needed food, rest, and a clean bandage; continual riding kept his wound irritated. He gritted his teeth and climbed and climbed, coming close to a gathering of boulders where the pitted sides of the mountain slanted down into a V shape. Would he find a pass or a great block of stone that would force him to turn and face his pursuers—worn and weakened, like a trapped wounded animal? The sun was down now and a mass of darkness scurried across the sky. His body slumped in the saddle, his eyes felt leaden with fatigue, but he could, in just a minute more of riding, lift in his stirrups and glimpse what lay at the bottom of the V shape.

He struggled to pull himself erect and stared. His eyes widened: it was a pass! A clean break between both sides of the mountain, a passage through. The Fargo luck had held out.

He glanced back; it would take the Larrabees at least a half-hour to reach this point and they wouldn't dare move through the pass on a moonless black night like this. No, they'd have to camp down. Even if they had a moon, they wouldn't dare traverse it—they'd be sitting ducks for his rifle fire. No, he could count on a full night of rest, time to eat, drink, and tend his wound. He took a deep breath and let the pinto move with instinctive sureness through the narrow gorge.

9

He was able to ride almost a half-mile between two towering mass of rocks before the black night rolled over him. A comfortable space behind a great boulder served for his camp area. He pulled off his shirt, then the blood-soaked bandages, replaced them with clean ones. Not daring to light a fire, he chewed remnant strips of beef jerky, drank from his canteen. He had grazed and watered the pinto a few times between his runs, and the horse looked in good shape. A night's rest would do both the horse and himself a world of good. He spread his bedroll, lay down, and felt a blissful sense of relief, ease to muscles that ached from hours and hours of riding. He pulled his gun, lay it near his hand, and stretched his muscles again. The heavy fatigue that dragged at him came, he believed, mostly from the seeping blood loss. No more jostling, at least for the next few hours. His eyelids, heavy as lead, closed, and he went instantly into a deep, dreamless sleep.

His eyes flicked open at the first touch of daylight, and he listened. Nothing human, only the sound of a flowing stream, muted with distance, and the cry of a hunting bird. He glanced at his arm: slight blood, mostly dried. He needed something in his gut before riding out, found hardtack in his saddlebag, and chewed it slowly.

The ground behind him was all clear between the great rising walls of stone. In front spread an immense verdant valley thick with cottonwood trees, bushes, stretches of tall grass. And he could see, happily, a small log cabin in the distance.

The sun was beginning its climb in what looked like a hot day when he reached the start of the valley. The sky then turned pink and pearl. At a rill, he let the pinto drink, refilled his canteens, and gazed back to the mountain gap, miles away. There they were, four horsemen, standing abreast, looking as if cast in stone. He stared hard at them and considered that it might help his cause if he could knock Conway out. He'd never shake this bunch with Conway as the lead man.

When he had shot at the posse, he had never found Conway for a clear-cut target; he had always managed to be behind someone, a tree, or on the ground. A shrewd joker, he never exposed himself, even when things looked peaceful. A touch of Indian in him, perhaps, like he himself, who was a quarter Cherokee.

He gazed ahead at the house in the gentle valley; it had a small wooden fence, a cow, and what looked like chickens. A quick stop there for some hot food and a word about where the hell he was. He had time for that, no matter how hot and heavy the Larrabees traveled.

The sun was a quarter up and the pinto was sweating when he reached the path to the house. It was small, the logs put together unevenly, sloppily, he thought; in fact, the carpenter work, the fence, window frames, all looked clumsy.

Then the window opened and a rifle barrel came out. "State your business, mister." A woman's voice, then he heard the low cry of a baby.

"I'm low on food. Would like to buy some eggs

and meat. I'll pay good money. Been traveling and come up short."

A long pause. "Where you been traveling from?"

"From Dakota Territory a while back. Came through that mountain, like to get my bearings. I'll just take the food and be on my way. You can put the food out and I'll leave the money, if you want."

Another long pause while the woman seemed to consider his words and probably her intuition. Women trust that most, he had learned long ago.

The barrel was pulled in, and then the door opened and a woman in an apron came to the door. She held the rifle while she studied his face, then lowered the weapon. "Right. Come into the house, I'll fix you some food."

"Thank you, ma'am." He tipped his hat, swung off the pinto and tied it to the fence.

Not much in the house: a thin table, two rickety chairs, an iron stove, a wooden bed, and a crib in which a baby with big blue eyes lay and gurgled.

"What would you want to eat? I'll fix it here. You might as well eat comfortable since you're paying."

He grinned. "Good, what have you got?"

She shrugged. "Eggs, chicken, milk, some beans."

He nodded. "I'll take all. What I can't eat now, I'll take with me." He put a double eagle on the table.

She looked at it. "That's a lot of money for what I'm giving you."

"Worth it to me. I need provisions."

She went toward the black iron stove.

He took a good look at her: an oval face, almost pretty, with pale skin, dark brown eyes, and a mouth that would be pretty if it wasn't so tightly pressed.

Where, he wondered, was her husband?

"There's a well in the back. You can wash if you want."

"Don't mind if I do." He pumped water into a basin, stripped his shirt, and scrubbed himself. The bandage showed only a small leakage of blood now; he must be healing. Thirty feet behind the house he noticed a recently dug grave with a wooden cross. Would that be her husband? He shook his head; if so, it left her in one hell of a setup. The house was too isolated for safety, and she couldn't stay here for any time without coming to grief. Not in rough territory like this, too many drifting desperadoes.

When he came back, he saw a sizzling chicken in a fry pan as well as a couple of eggs. A big glass of milk on the table made him smile, something he hadn't drunk in a while. He'd drink it now, instead of whiskey; certainly it'd be less threatening to her. She would have to be leery of strangers, and he took it as a compliment that she had sized him up as worthy of trust.

The baby gurgled happily at the sight of him and threw its plump arms around; he leaned down and smiled at it, held out his finger, which the baby grabbed and held tightly. It was a girl baby, with golden curly hair and a cute little face.

"That's a good-looking baby."

She looked at it, and her face tightened, then she smiled. "She's very good, she's very sweet."

A bit like the mother, he thought, but said nothing.

She soon had the eggs out in a dish, and let the chicken pieces continue to fry. She cut two thick pieces of bread, buttered them, and put them beside his eggs. Then she poured two cups of coffee and joined him at the table.

As he ate with gusto, she watched, drank her own coffee, and his appetite seemed to amuse her. "You're hungry enough. It's nice to see a man eat."

He nodded and felt his strength growing.

"What's your name?" she asked.

"Skye Fargo. And yours?"

"Millie Stewart."

"Mrs. Stewart, I should think you'd be seeing a man eat every day. Your husband."

"He's dead," she said tonelessly. "Died two months ago. That's him in the back. You must have seen it."

"I did. What happened? I mean, how'd he die, if I'm not too inquisitive, ma'am?"

She shook her head. "He died chopping a tree, for God's sake. A heart attack. Dead. He had a bad heart, but didn't know it, that's what Doc Riley said. Poor Dennis, he wasn't much of a builder, but he wanted so badly to be one. I could have built this house better than him, but didn't dare. He'd of skinned me, he had so much pride. That was his trouble, he was all pride, and a bad heart. Didn't know how to take it easy. And this is a hard life around here."

Fargo shook his head; it was a lousy situation, a woman alone like this.

"Not planning to stay, are you?"

"No. My father's on his way. Be here in the next three days. We're from Fremont—that's thirty miles north."

Fremont. Wasn't that where Abigail wanted to go, where her folks came from? Curious coincidence, he thought.

"You're smart to leave this place. It's raw country for a woman alone." He rubbed his chin. "I'm not clear on my whereabouts. What do I hit if I continue west?"

She smiled. "You hit Ruby Carson's place, and the trail from there takes you to Spoon River. All that is west."

He stared. Damn, he almost sensed that. Through the gap in the mountain, a giant circle took him back to Ruby's place, and could take him, if he was interested in a visit to hell, back to the Larrabee ranch. At least he knew the lay of the land and would not be riding blind anymore.

"We came out here to start a family and a home. I've got part of the family." Millie smiled at the baby, already asleep. "But that's it. Dad hated the idea of us coming here. 'Stay in town,' he said, 'the life will be easier. Out in the wild you'll have to start from scratch, cut lumber, build a house, tend animals dawn to dark.' " She sighed. "But Dennis wanted to set up his own life, his land, his home. He just didn't have the heart. Dead two months." Her eyes stayed steady on him. "A long time."

"I'm sorry about your trouble," he said. "A man must know his limits. By the way, ever meet Abigail Larrabee?"

She nodded. "Oh, yes. She came from my town. She was Abigail Sanders back there. A fine young woman, we all loved her. She could have the pick of men and she ups and marries Matty Larrabee. Oh, he was handsome and one of the rich Larrabees, but under his front he was a spoiled kid, though he looked like a man. She should have showed more sense."

He smiled. Marriage was a blind game, you

130

didn't know what you had until the unmasking much later.

Millie cocked her head. "You know Abigail?"

"Yes, I do have an acquaintance with her. A proper young lady."

"Proper, yes, and she can shoot a squirrel's butt at fifty yards. I've seen her," Millie said.

She got up, looked at the chicken frying in the pan, pushed it around, went to the baby, fixed its covers, looked sadly down at it, probably, Fargo thought, thinking of the baby as fatherless. She came back and poured some coffee in his cup and hers.

"Chicken smells good," he said.

"I can cook all right, but there's no one to cook for. Can't wait to get out of here."

"Won't be long. You'll be with your folks again. You'll meet some good man." He felt a bit uneasy; he wanted to be polite, especially to a woman like her, who'd suffered the loss of a husband and who was good enough to cook for him and had a bag of misery just now. But he had a lynch gang on his heels. He glanced out the window, but couldn't see anything, just the pinto.

She followed his glance. "That's a fine horse you've got. Never saw one quite that powerful."

Fargo smiled. She'd hit a tender point of pride. "Never a horse like him. The best."

She, too, smiled at his pride. "Looks like he'd been running a lot; it's a rotten hot day."

"Yes, I've been working him hard. Coming through the mountain is rough going."

She shook her head. "You're the first man who ever came through the mountainside. Must have lost your bearings. And it's a devil-hard climb. Not a good idea to push a horse that hard on a day like this."

What was she after? All this concern for the pinto. "He can take it."

She shrugged. "Never know what a man or animal can take. Poor Dennis didn't know how much he could take." She sighed. "Dead two months." She looked at him, smiled curiously. "To tell the truth, Fargo, I miss not having a man."

Her eyes held on his, steady—they were dark, soft eyes, and they were not ashamed of what she was feeling. She was lonely, used to having a man, she now burned with the passion of a healthy young woman. She had a nice figure and her breasts were heavy.

"I think I know what you mean, Millie."

She pointed to the low wooden bed. "That bed at night is the loneliest place in the world. And every night it gets worse. I miss Dennis terribly. And I miss the lovin'. It's natural to miss lovin' when you had it for a good long time. And so, half the night I mourn Dennis, and half the night I burn . . . with desire."

There were four men miles away, coming at him, hellbent to hang him. And Millie, here, wanted him to stop and give her lovin'. Could he do a thing like that? It'd be like screwing under a hangman's noose! But could he pass it up? She had a lovely mouth and a great pair of breasts.

"Stay awhile," she said, "Your horse can use the rest."

He felt a great surge of desire, and then he thought again of the Larrabees.

"You don't want to," she said. There was pain in her face.

"I want to, Millie. Very much. But I must tell you this: I'm on the run. I've done nothing bad, and it's the truth. But there are four men hot on my trail. And they mean me mischief."

"Where are they?" she demanded.

He smiled. "They're coming. But I've got a safety margin of twenty minutes. Twenty minutes. I can give you all the lovin' I got in that time. If you want it. And then I've got to run."

She stared at him, at his face, then at his body, and she saw his bulge; that pushed her over. She flung her apron over her head and began to pull at the buttons of her dress. He stared at her, frozen, and she gaped at him, then yelled, "What the hell are you waiting for?"

He grinned and went into action. In two minutes, they were facing each other, nude.

Her breasts, as he guessed, were magnificent: full, plump, round, with hard, erect nipples. Her tummy was softly rounded, her legs finely shaped, and there was fleecy dark hair between her thighs.

Her eyes widened at sight of his bigness; she gasped for breath; then, as if a devil took hold, she flung herself on her knees in front of him, grabbed him, rubbed her face against his swollen excitement like an uncontrolled animal in heat. Then she took him into the warmth; her lips moved and the rage of her hunger filled him with wonder. He watched her in her frenzies and she seemed to soar into her climax, one after another; then she let go, pulled him to the bed on top of her. He slipped into her smooth warmth, and her body lunged with frantic rhythm, and again she soared to a towering excitement, moaning and groaning, as if some diabolic spirit had delivered her to the torments of hell. Her movements, wild and fierce, brought him to an overpowering surge. And her body, still diabolically inspired, kept writhing and writhing as his own passion expired.

Now he lay dull and dreamy on her heaving body, then his flesh crawled as he heard the fearful neigh of his pinto.

He knew the meaning of the sound. His eyes snapped open, and still nude, he grabbed his gun and raced to the window. A sidewinder, thick and long, slithered two feet from the tethered horse; it stamped and pulled in a state of mortal fear. Fargo's gun spit twice and the rattlesnake jumped, twisted in agony, curled and twisted, and slowly died.

He looked toward the mountain; they were coming, the four of them, riding furiously; they were probably close enough to see the pinto tied outside the house.

He literally dived into his clothes, grabbed the chicken from the fry pan, kissed her as she still lay on the bed; her eyes looked as big as saucers.

"Twenty minutes are gone," he said, and streaked for the door.

She got up on one elbow, and as he went out the door, she was still staring.

He threw the chicken into a pouch, untied the pinto, and kicked aside the rattler, its eyes glazed with death. He swung over the saddle and went galloping across the valley.

He glanced over his shoulder and smiled. They had been running their horses all out, hoping to nail him at the house, but with that hope now gone, they eased up on the running. One thing would be clear in Terry's head: they could never catch the pinto from behind. They'd just have to plug and try and wear him down, or hope for some miracle.

He rode northwest at a steady pace, unwilling to push hard. The pinto had to be skittish from its encounter with the snake. It was past noon, the sun beat down fiercely and the sky shone like a polished dish. But the valley looked lush and green, with its great trees and its spreading branches that cast cool shade.

The terrain for the next three hours didn't change much and finally Fargo stopped at a stream. The pinto drank. He washed up, filled his canteen, sat against the trunk of a cottonwood, and ate the fried chicken.

Chewing the tender meat, he smiled, thinking of Millie. That had to be the hungriest woman he ever met. It was a pity and a shame that Dennis up and died on her, her needing a man that much. She was a hell of a woman, but maybe she tore off like that because she had just twenty minutes. Sure beat hell out of the deadline, he thought with a grin. And, damn, her chicken was really delicious. With all her talents, Millie would have no trouble getting another husband.

He wondered what the Larrabees did about food. Live game, probably, but they had to hunt it and stop to eat it. But Terry would keep the pressure on, he must thrive on the thought of revenge. Well, Terry did have grievances; in his eyes Fargo had violated two Larrabee women, he dared invade the Bar-L ranch in a phony masquerade, and on this wild run he had put a lot of Larrabee men out. Terry had strung up men, probably, for a tenth of such offenses.

Fargo chuckled. It gave him a kick to have Terry in such a roaring rage. Still, it was no laughing matter. There'd be four guns against him if he made one slip, and slips did happen. You never knew when fate might start to pelt

you with manure; he'd seen it happen often
enough.

He stroked his chin, a bit annoyed at himself
for such negative ideas. If you thought negative,
it always seemed to happen.

He flicked the chicken bones into the air,
climbed on the pinto, and cantered west.

According to Millie, the trail west would spin
him past Ruby's. Well, he didn't care about Ruby,
but he did want to get closer to Abigail. He had
made a decision to help her and felt committed
to it. He hadn't the vaguest idea yet how, but it
would be stupid to barrel-ass into the Bar-L and
try to pull her out. But if he put himself nearby,
he might luck into something.

He glanced back. They were about three miles
away and pushing the horses. He scowled. Only
three of them. Who was missing? Conway! Where
in hell did he go? When? A stab of tension. This
came from mind-wandering, taking everything
for granted, thinking they would just follow, dumb
and dogged. Well, they had thought of an angle.
Conway—why him? He was the shrewdest, the
cleverest, the tracker. It meant that they had
doped out his direction and that Conway knew
how to short-circuit it, cut him off. Maybe stop
and pick up manpower.

All this came from his promise to help Abigail.
If he were to turn sharp east, he'd avoid a helluva
lot of trouble. East was clear running, west was
ambush, the closing of a ring. Any sensible man
would choose east.

So why'd he choose to ride, eyes open, into a
trap? Because of a young woman with golden
hair and cobalt-blue eyes who'd looked at him
with such hope, who needed his help to escape

from a miserable life with a drunk, vicious Larrabee, and from Terry, who insisted she live with her misery.

The look of the land became familiar, the cottonwoods, the dense bushes, the scattered rocks, the sort of land that surrounded Spoon River.

The Larrabees, he noted, were spurring their horses. Did it mean they wanted to close the distance between them, or to push him pell-mell into a trap? From here on, he should stay keyed up and expect ambush. He wouldn't spur the pinto, not yet. Even if the Larrabees closed in, he would still keep a margin of safety.

He rode carefully, as the sun slid down and the air cooled. Although nothing had happened, he still stayed mobilized. He had reached the trail near Ruby's place, and behind him, at least a mile, the Larrabees were pounding hard; they had, for some reason, picked up speed.

He suddenly sensed something, and he stared at the large bush to the right of him and the big boulder opposite it. The bush quivered, as if touched by the wind, but there was no wind. His instincts screamed and his gun barked at the same time that he heard another gun, and the bullet whined past his ear. He fired again, heard a groan. Then, something behind the rock moved, and to deflect any aim, he fired, turned the pinto toward Ruby's, put him all out, firing back again. A glimpse of a face from behind the rock—he fired, saw bone and flesh slashed off by his bullet. Though the Larrabees were pounding in, they were still too far for guns. He raced up the big lawn in front of the big white house, came off the pinto on a run, crouched low, and went to the door.

Ruby, startled by the fusillade of shots, was coming to the door. She saw it open, and the big, lean, square-faced man with lake-blue eyes, gun drawn, came in.

"Hello, Ruby," Fargo said, smiling, but his cool eyes did not quite match the smile.

10

Though Ruby was startled by the gunfire near her house, it didn't seem to diminish her pleasure at seeing Fargo. Her eyes glittered as if she was hit by memories of a good time, her Cupid's-bow mouth smiled, and then she looked at his gun.

"What is happening, Clancy? What's the gun for?"

He looked through the window. "You'll probably be as surprised about this as I am, Ruby, but some men out there are trying to kill me."

She frowned. "I hope not. It would be a serious loss to the world of women. But you must be funning."

"Dead serious," he said.

"And who would be trying that?" She moved nearer.

"I think you should stay back, Miss Ruby, in case they fire through the window. I wouldn't want you hurt."

She didn't move. "Who's out there?" Who would dare shoot into this house?"

"I hate to say this, but it might be friends of yours. The Larrabees."

She stared at him. "Why would they want to shoot you, Clancy? What have you done?"

"The name's Fargo, Miss Ruby. It's not Clancy."

"What do you mean? What *is* all this?" She studied him. "Are you wanted? Why did you use a false name?"

"It's a long story, honey, and I'm not sure it would interest you."

Her lips tightened. "It interests me, all right, Mr. Fargo. You're on my property. And I don't like anyone barging in here with a gun. And maybe getting my place all shot up. Now, what's all this about?"

He kept his eye on the window, but no one appeared. "You'll never believe it," he said, glancing at her.

She was wearing, as usual, a low-cut dress that revealed a lot of her queen-sized breasts; her black eyes were shadowed, her lush auburn hair flowed to her shoulders, and her sensual figure filled her dress with spectacular effect.

She caught his appreciative look and couldn't help smiling. A woman like her enjoyed the looks of men. "Tell me"—her voice was less strident—"I may believe it, Clancy or Fargo. I find it hard to believe you've done something wrong to the Larrabees. You don't seem to be the kind."

He studied the front of the house, looked out the side windows, and strangely, they didn't seem ready to tackle him—at least not yet. Holding a strategy meeting? Maybe, they didn't like the idea of barging in on Ruby Carson. Whatever the reason, it looked like a helluva peaceful scene just now.

"Want some whiskey, Fargo?" she smiled. "If there's one thing I've got plenty of, it's whiskey." She had decided to be genial. She felt the whiskey might loosen his tongue. He smiled inwardly. "María," she called.

"Who's in the house?" he asked quickly.

"My girl María, that's about it."

"How about the men?"

"Two men are usually in the house for odd jobs, but they're out just now."

María, a well-fed dark woman, appeared; she looked frightened. "Bring some whiskey for us, and two glasses. And take it easy, María. Mr. Fargo here is a friend."

María's black eyes shone, she flashed her teeth and looked nervously at his gun. When she brought the whiskey on a tray with two glasses, she flashed her teeth again, then made a fast exit.

Ruby poured and gave him a full glass.

He took a sip. She was right, it was good whiskey. But good or not, it wasn't about to loosen his tongue.

His position near the window gave him a commanding view. To get near that door, they'd have to traverse twenty yards of lawn, and he'd have to be blind to miss them.

Nothing stirred out there. He figured they were jolted at his move and were trying to work out something. They had to treat Ruby gently, she with her moneybags, and they didn't think it smart to come stomping in and blasting up her house. It looked for the moment like a real standoff.

He liked that. He took another sip from the glass.

She smiled and poured some more.

"Now, Fargo, perhaps you will finally satisfy my curiosity. Why are the Larrabees so mad at you?"

He dragged a chair to the window, took a spot that gave him the largest view to any approach to the house, plunked his bulk down. "You're not drinking," Ruby said. "Didn't you build up a big thirst with all that running, honey?"

She smiled, wanting to make sure the whiskey would do its job, loosening him up. She came closer, her hips moving sensually; she stood near him, and she smelled real nice. He reached out and patted one of her round buttocks; she certainly had a great bottom.

Her dark eyes gleamed. "For a man out to defend his life, you don't seem to be thinking too hard about it."

"It's hard thinking when you're nearby, Ruby," he said. "Always like a beautiful woman around. If a man's gotta go, what other way than in the company of a good-looking woman?"

She shook her head, as if astonished at his coolness under seige. "Maybe you don't have to go. Now, what's this all about?"

It wasn't because of the whiskey that his blood flowed warm and his fatigue seemed gone. He felt comfortable, even chatty. Nothing to worry about just now. He'd thrown a block on the Larrabees with this inspired run into Ruby's. He could picture them out there, huddling heads, trying to figure out the next move.

Ruby had a gimlet eye on him, waiting to have the mystery cleared up.

"Well," he drawled, "you may not realize this, Ruby, but you are the cause of all my woes."

She didn't think his remark amusing. "Are you drunk already? That's not funny."

"Not funny, but true. Let me tell you a little story. I was passing through Spoon River about a week ago, on my way to Devil's Crossing. Got tired and hot and lay down under a big oak for forty winks. Three good-looking women, with guns, woke me from my sweet slumber." He told her the whole story of the Larrabee women and Terry's executioners. While he told it, he kept a sharp eye on the lawn and allowed himself another sip of the liquor.

She never took her eyes from him; they were big with fascination.

"So, Ruby, I found out that the ladies, to revenge themselves, grabbed a man passing through. Me." He smiled. "Here's where you come in. It seems the husbands were pleasuring themselves too often with a lady named Ruby. That's why this sticky mess started."

She was speechless, digesting the story.

He grinned. "You're not to blame, of course. It's Terry who started the shooting. But by my count, there are about ten men either dead or wounded."

Ruby looked as though a dozen thoughts were spinning in her head. Her lips curled and her smile was definitely not nice. "Those Larrabee women, always giving themselves airs. They're no better'n anyone else. Acting so high and mighty."

She stopped and started to walk back and forth, as if excited by her thoughts. "At least, I don't hold a gun on a man to get him," she snarled. She stopped, stared with hostile eyes at him. "Are you telling me it's my fault, those men?" she demanded.

"No, I say it's Terry's. He's a hard man, wants his satisfaction. Gotta have my hide. But I don't like that idea at all."

She looked tough as nails, stared at the window as if hoping someone would be there. He shot a glance out also, but saw no one.

Her face was a study, then her mouth hardened.

"Listen, Fargo, or whatever your name is, I want you to get the hell out of here."

He smiled; there was obviously a lot happening in her head. "That's not ladylike talk, Ruby. I'm sure you don't want me to go out there. Get a bunch of lead thrown at me."

"I don't care. It's not my fault. Why'd you come here?"

" 'Fraid I was forced here, Ruby. They blocked the trail."

She looked downright ugly. "Well, you can't stay here. I don't want you here."

His eyes narrowed. "You don't seem to understand, little lady. I'm here till I'm ready to go. And you've got nothing to say about it."

She looked startled. "What do you mean? What are you going to do?"

"Nothing at the moment. Just rest easy."

"I don't want to rest easy." She thought for a moment. "I'm going out there."

He grinned. "No, Ruby. I like your company. I'd like you to stay."

"You can't keep me here. I'll call Terry."

He laughed. "Go ahead. Nothing I'd like better than a clear look at him."

Her eyes glinted balefully and she walked to the window and, somewhat to his surprise, began to call out, "Terry! Terry! Come and get me, honey. This low-down skunk won't let me leave."

Silence.

"Terry, do you hear me?"

Another silence. Terry hears you, but he'd rather not, Fargo thought.

Then Terry's voice came from behind a huge boulder about thirty yards in front of the clearing that led to Ruby's house.

"Are you all right, Ruby? He hasn't hurt you?"

"I'm all right," she called. "But he won't let me leave. Teach him a lesson, Terry."

A pause. "Don't worry, we'll take good care of Fargo. Just sit tight for a while." Another pause. "Maybe you can make yourself useful, honey."

She stared out, as if by looking hard enough she could see through the boulder, then turned and took a long gulp of her whiskey. Fargo grinned. She seemed let down that her hero Terry didn't come charging up like a bull to rescue his darling. Well, he wasn't a complete lunatic.

"Am I your prisoner," she asked finally.

"I just want you to stick around. I think Terry values your health. That makes you a bargaining chip."

"What do you mean, bargaining chip?"

"Well, if he doesn't want you hurt, he won't want me hurt."

Her lip curled. "I didn't think that was your style. Hiding behind a woman's skirt."

He grinned. "I'd rather hide under them."

Her eyes widened at his remark, then she clenched her teeth, started to pace from one end of the room to the other. She was nervous, and he felt he could read her thoughts. She had a big investment in Terry and the Bar-L, and wanted nothing happening to it. She could almost taste the pleasure of being Mrs. Terry Larrabee. It made her skittish to think she'd lose all that if Terry went down in a gunfight. Fargo was the enemy: he'd barged into their lives and he might ruin her best-laid plans. Yes, Fargo was the enemy and better off dead.

The flow of feelings over her face told Fargo that the sexy lady had become the deadly lady.

Her eyes gleamed with cunning, and he thought it would be smart to expect a low blow.

"It'd be nice, Fargo, if nobody got hurt. More whiskey?"

"No, thanks." He grinned. She still imagined that booze would turn him stupid. She didn't know how he handled it.

She filled her glass again and stood close, brushing him with her body. Her perfume hit him; there was certainly a sizzle in the lady. He put his hand on her bottom. What the hell, enemy or not, she was still a fine piece of flesh. That curvy behind was nice to caress.

She was one hot lady, all right, always ready to purr if you stroked. She smiled, bringing her big white breasts near his face. He shifted so that the curve of her bosom did not block his view, then he tugged at her dress and one breast jumped out, its pink nipple pouting.

He nuzzled it; whiskey and tit were an unbeatable mix, he thought. He put his tongue to it teasingly, and she said, "Oh, Fargo, you were meant for lovin', not killin'."

We all are, he thought, but there had to be a lot of Terrys in the world who spoiled things.

He lifted her dress, smoothed his hand up her sleek thigh. Nothing underneath, he realized, astonished. His hand touched her fleecy pubic hair, he drew his finger lightly over the warm crease, eased in; it felt juicy warm. He played a bit, heard her breathing go heavy. It hit him funny, this setup, he with a gun in one hand while his other touched her right on the button. Then she went tight, grabbed his head, pulled it to her body, cutting off his vision. It was natural, and he gently pulled back for a clear view. He had put the spurs to her passion, and she wanted more. She slipped to her knees, dug at his britches, got his flesh out, ponderous and alert. She leaned into it with that Cupid's-bow mouth and loved it tender and fierce. She did it long and lustfully, then hiked up her dress and, facing him, sat down. Her big breasts swung in his face as her hips squirmed and squirmed. This, it hit him, had to be a deadly time; if Terry and his men dropped by, he'd be a goner. But they didn't, and the danger instead spiced his pleasure. She squirmed and squirmed, and he didn't give a damn about the Larrabees or anything else. All he wanted was to hit the peak; then he felt himself thicken, swell, and explode. Ruby's body, as if on signal, seemed to convulse, and she let out a strangled scream.

Silence.

Then he heard the sound, the whisper of wood, and he pushed her and fired at the door. She grabbed at his pistol hand, but he shoved her, amazed that he was still in her. He pulled away, crawled fast and flat across the floor to the window to peer out. A man there, on the ground, raising his gun. They both fired, and the whine of a bullet went past his head, splintered the wall. His bullet speared the man's skull, leaving a red gaping hole.

It was Conway.

Conway, that hound dog, had managed somehow to crawl on his belly at a sharp angle to the house until he'd reached the front door. He seemed to know it would be safe, that Fargo would be all wrapped up in Ruby.

So how'd he know? How could he know that Ruby would have him paralyzed with sex? "Make yourself useful, honey," that was it! That son of a bitch Terry. Those were code words and Ruby would understand. It meant throw your crotch at Fargo, tie him up, and Terry would do the rest. Only it was Conway who got it. That bitch Ruby! She was fumbling in the desk, trying to grab something. It took one leap to reach her, twist the small pistol from her hands, and push her. She fell against the wall.

Damn, that was a pisser. Proved the cheating heart of some women. That Ruby, she used her crotch like a weapon, and it almost worked. One thing about screwing, it sure turned a man's mind to mush.

Now he'd have to tie her, for she couldn't be trusted.

When he called María, she came in timidly, her black eyes shining. He gave her a broad grin. "Nothing to worry about, María. I'm mighty hungry. Rustle up some grub for us. And bring some rope."

She nodded quickly, then threw a fearful look at Ruby sitting quietly in the chair.

"Pronto," he said.

She hurried to the kitchen.

The view from the window looked peaceful, except for Conway. Poor Conway, he'd made the mistake of picking the wrong boss. It was shrewd the way Terry, to get his dirty work done, put everyone else in the way of a bullet. He was tough, clever, and dangerous. What the hell would be his next move? He seemed always to have one. Couldn't rush the door, that would be suicidal. He played an ace with Ruby as the sex decoy. What was left? Could it be a stalemate?

Not with Terry. He had a lot in the pot, all those dead and wounded men. And the Larrabee women violated by Fargo, that was the deepest cut of all, the unforgivable insult.

So, what would Terry do? He didn't have much choice, and that seemed the plain truth. He wanted Ruby whole, because she was his money-bag. He'd have to trade, sooner or later. Ruby with a whole skin in exchange for Fargo with free passage. But Terry was tricky, and maybe he had a move: it was like a game of chess.

From her chair, Ruby watched him, eyes like a lynx. She'd come to realize that in the conflict of two men, she was the pawn, and she didn't like it. He pulled the table to the window so that when the food came, he could eat and keep an eye out.

María brought in two steaks, black-eyed peas, biscuits, and coffee, and put the crusty brown, double-thick slab in front of him. He cut a piece, chewed it with gusto, forked the beans, stuffed his mouth with buttered biscuits. He had wolfed down half the steak before he noticed Ruby's food was untouched.

"Sorry you're not hungry."

She glared. "Hard to be hungry with a dead man lying outside my door."

He thought of Conway, not a bad cowboy, but the fact was that he had sneaked up on that door with mean intent.

"Oh, that." He shrugged. "Life must go on. Stomachs keep getting empty. Gotta eat." He cut another tender slice, forked it into his mouth, gulped coffee. Everything tasted fine. "Great cook, that María."

Ruby toyed with her fork, decided then to try

a piece of meat, and after chewing it, tried another. Her mood seemed to brighten a bit.

"Fargo," she said with a grimace, "I don't see how you're going to get out of this."

"Well, I'll give it a try."

"There's nowhere you can go. You're trapped here. Sooner or later, you've got to give up."

He gave her an innocent look. "Do you think I should?"

She leaned forward. "Yes, I do. To avoid more bloodshed."

He nodded, as if her point was logical, cut another piece of steak. "I guess a hanging does avoid bloodshed." He shook his head. "No, after all, it's not a good idea. Terry's an unforgiving man."

"I'll talk to him. He might listen to reason."

He smiled brightly. "What would you say?"

"I'd say ..." She frowned, thinking hard. "I'd say that you could have hurt me, but that you didn't. That's the main thing."

He glanced outside, everything peaceful. "I think that's reasonable. And what would he say?"

She threw him a spiteful look. "What do you mean? There's only one thing he could say. He doesn't want me hurt."

He grinned broadly. "That's what I'm counting on, Miss Ruby. You mean a lot to him. He wouldn't want you hurt. So, it comes to this: he's got to let me go, if I let you go."

She scowled. "But you don't have me."

"Oh, yes, I've got you."

"I'm in this house with you. But you don't have me," she said irritably.

"María," he called.

She came, looking pale.

"I told you to get rope, where is it?"

She nodded, went quickly to the kitchen, and came back with a piece of line. He slashed it to the right length. Suddenly he grabbed Ruby's hands, held her wrists, and though she put up a struggle, he tied them snugly together.

He gave her a bright smile. "If you're still hungry, Ruby, honey, I'll feed you. Just like a baby. Fork the food into your mouth."

"Go to hell."

He looked agreeably at her, cut another piece of meat, and chewed it. "Mmm. Nothing like having a beautiful woman tied and in your power. Brings out the beast in a man."

"You sound like a low-down skunk," she snarled.

"Who me?" His voice was innocent. "Who was it got me all hot and bothered so the man outside could sneak up and potshot me? Why'd you do that?"

Her teeth gritted. "Because I wanted them to shoot your head off," she hissed.

"Why, honey? What have I done to you, except play when you wanted? I was your playmate and you want me shot. That's not nice, Ruby. I don't think, after all, that you're a nice girl." He shook his head. "No, you're not. Shoulda listened to my auntie when I was a chitling. She told me, beware of a dark-eyed, strange woman." He finished his steak, drank the coffee, and stood.

"Whyn't you go upstairs and rest. I'll let you know if anything good is happening. Wish I could join you, but I gotta keep an eye on things." He lifted her, carried her to the stairs.

She glared, then stomped up angrily.

He stretched his long legs, tilted back in the chair. He was in no sweat. He had Ruby, and the

Larrabees were huddled behind that boulder, no doubt racking their brains about it.

To keep himself from being bored, he ran back in his mind the string of events that put him in this house under seige.

He'd been minding his own business, on his way to Devil's Crossing only a week ago, when the three gunwomen stopped him and started this crazy circus of screwing and shooting. Ruby, in a way, had triggered his misfortunes, as he told her, but fate was playing a joke. Because it was the Larrabee women who, because they craved revenge, dragged him in and set off the chain of wild events. Death and destruction then came to Scarface and his sidekicks, to a lot of Larrabee men, and to Conway, who lay sprawled on the other side of that door.

"Hey, Fargo." Terry's voice.

"Yeah."

"We don't like Conway lying there like that."

"So what?"

"We'd like to pick him up."

Fargo smiled. It wasn't in character for Terry to be that kindhearted.

"What you got in mind?"

"I'll send Matty over. He'll pick up Conway. Then maybe he'll powwow with you. How about it?"

"Let him come."

It took five minutes before Matty came from behind the boulder and started toward the house. His big bulk, a Larrabee body, moved slowly, and he smiled, as if he was on a visit to a friend.

Fargo watched with slitted eyes. He had to keep in mind that he was the guest of honor of a Larrabee lynch party, and that Matty had been riding with it.

Matty walked carefully, his eyes on the window where Fargo sat, gun in hand. When he reached the dead Conway, he stopped, looked down a long moment, then turned.

"Say, Clancy, I mean, Fargo, I'm sure sorry about all this. Hope we can straighten it out without anyone else getting hurt. We sure don't want Ruby hurt. And I got no beef about you. Listen, I'm just gonna carry Conway out to our people, then I want to come and talk. Will that be all right, Fargo?"

"Sure. Take Conway and come back."

Matty lifted the dead man and carried him off. There seemed to be more men on the trail, for he heard voices, the sound of horses. Probably taking Conway for burying.

Matty came back, stood outside the door, took off his stetson. His red hair glowed in the late sun.

"Can I come in, Fargo?"

"Open the door."

He came in, his broad handsome face smiling. He looked curiously at Fargo, at the gun in his hand. He was not wearing a gun.

Fargo studied Matty for a moment, his empty holster, his face, his body, then put his Colt in its holster. The bottle caught Matty's eye. "Damn, I've got a great thirst. How about it?" Fargo nodded, and watched the man turn the bottle up and take a long pull. "Damn, I needed that." He grinned. "You led us a bitch of a run, Fargo, damn you. Never saw a horse work like your pinto. Must have an iron heart."

"He's got that."

Matty took another pull, and booze vanished down his throat. He wiped his mouth.

"Tell you, Fargo, I never thought we'd get you. Till Conway figured out how to bypass you, get in front." He laughed. "But he sure picked the world's worst place. Drove you right into Ruby's! And that must be the most stupid trick that could have happened." He leaned forward. "See, Fargo, Ruby's important to us Larrabees. Tell you the truth, she practically owns half the Bar-L. Her money. We were going down, and Terry didn't like that, so he picks up with Ruby. He liked her anyway, and she liked him. And so she bailed us out. We don't want anything to happen to her. That's how you lucked in, Fargo, coming here."

He pulled again at the whiskey. "Like mother's milk." He grinned, his voice thickened. "Wanna tell you, Fargo, I got nuthin' against you. You did nuthin' against me. It was Maude and Julia pulled that stunt. And you saved my hide from the big bad Bronc. So, far as I'm concerned, you're four aces."

He ran his hand through his red hair. " 'Course, you did a lot of damage to our men. That goddamn rifle of yours—it shoots a mile, don't it?" He grinned drunkenly. "But it's hard to blame you. Didn't think much of the idea of lynching, did you?" He slapped his knee as if it was a very funny idea. "That damned Terry, he's a hard man," he said, and finished the bottle. He looked at the stairs. "Ruby up there, I guess?"

"Yeah, Ruby's upstairs, you drunken brat." It was Ruby's voice on the stairs. She came down, her eyes glittering. "You got a big mouth, Matty, and one day it's gonna get you a fast funeral."

He stared amazed. "Whadda I say? Look, honey, I'm here to get you off the hook."

She glared. "Well, let's hear it, not a lot of loose talk about my money."

He looked hurt. "Now I didn't say anything bad, honey. You're a lucky lady, you gotta lot of money. Anything wrong with that?"

She looked disgusted. "Listen, you dumb lummox. Why are you here? What's Terry going to do?"

Matty scratched his head. "Damn, didn't I tell that? We're going to swap. You go out. Fargo goes free. So nobody gets hurt."

Fargo scowled. "Draw that picture a little better."

"I mean, you bring her out, and we swear to let you go," Matty said.

Fargo laughed. "Are you simpleminded? This is how it goes: I take her out in front of me; I got a gun on her. She's my guarantee. Anyone makes a move, she's gone. If you don't chase, I'll turn her loose in ten minutes."

Matty thought about it, then he nodded and a strange smile twisted his face. "That's fine, that's okay. That's really what Terry figured you'd want. So it's a deal."

"A deal," Fargo said. He watched Matty put on his stetson and stagger. It struck him that Matty was too drunk for the small amount he'd taken. But he did have a weak head. Matty staggered to the door, grinned, turned, tried to tip his hat, it fell. He swore and groped for it. As Fargo watched, Matty's hand sneaked under his pants leg, came out with a derringer, pointed at Fargo. But Fargo's own hand moved like a streak and he fired from the hip, his bullet piercing the forehead, spattering Matty's brains against the door. Matty was dead before he hit the floor.

* * *

It happened so fast that Ruby seemed to go into shock. She stood frozen, her eyes staring, her hands on her breasts, and she would have screamed if she could have found her voice.

"Damned idiot," Fargo growled. Everything Matty did, he did wrong; there were men like that, born under an evil star. He had enough booze in him to thicken his thinking, and he imagined he could pull a gun from his boot, one of the oldest tricks, and get away with it. Well, he should have died before, with a bullet from Bronco. So he lived a few extra days, but men like him were meant for a short and stupid life.

Ruby's eyes were on Fargo, spewing hate and fear. She was going to spit some poison at him. And she did. "You rotten bastard, you killed him." The sexy lady obviously hadn't seen the derringer.

"I think so," Fargo said. "I suppose you'd rather he killed me?"

Her lips twisted, her voice was shrill. "How could he? He had no gun. You killed him in cold blood."

When Matty toppled, his body covered the derringer, and she could only see his back. With the point of his boot, Fargo pulled Matty's hand from under his body—it clutched the gun.

"What's this?" Fargo asked.

It took a full minute for her to piece it all together. "But where'd it come from?"

"Inside his boot."

She looked bewildered and stared at Matty's body with all sorts of feelings. Probably she had special memories.

Fargo shot a glance outside. The Larrabees had to have some anxious moments, wondering who got the bullet. They were hoping to hear Matty's voice.

Ruby shook her head. "I just don't understand what happened."

"I'll tell you what happened. Matty came in with an empty holster to prove he was peaceful. He drank a lot of booze to prove he was drunk. He talked a lot of bull to phony a deal. Then, when he thought he had me hog-tied, he pulled his hidden gun."

Her gaze stayed with fascinated terror on the sprawled body. "But why'd he try it? There was a deal. All he had to do was tell Terry."

Fargo shrugged. "Wanted to be the hero. Prove to his brothers that he could do what they couldn't. Nail me. The kid finally proved himself."

She looked at the empty bottle as if she could use a drink. "Poor Matty. He had his faults, but I liked him. I still don't know why he tried it."

"He's a Larrabee," Fargo said with a tight smile.

"Now what? I can't stand it, him lying there."

He leaned on the window and called. "Terry."

There was a long silence.

He smiled. They must have been hoping against hope it would be Matty's voice. They'd heard the gunshot, and until this moment they didn't know whose gun. Now they knew, and it would take time to digest. They couldn't be feeling good.

"Yeah," Terry finally said.

"Matty's dead." He waited a beat. "He pulled a gun. His mistake, because we had a deal. A deal with nobody getting hurt."

Again a long silence. A brother dead, not easy to take.

"What was the deal, Fargo?" The voice was guttural.

"I'll talk to Abigail."

"Why?"

"She's lost her man. She's gotta know. I'll give her the deal."

"All right, Fargo." Terry's voice was choked with rage.

Fargo pulled out a cheroot. All he wants is my head in a rope, he thought.

11

The sight of Matty lying there upset Ruby, and after a few moments she climbed the stairs.

Fargo went to the window. "Terry."

"Yeah."

"Send Luke to pick up Matty. Luke without guns. Without guns. Is that clear?"

"Yeah."

Luke, when he came out, looked huge, bullish, and even though his holster was empty, he was a threatening presence. Fargo, taking no chances, kept his gun out to discourage any wrong move.

Luke pushed the door open, stared with a masklike face at Matty, at the derringer in his hand, then picked up the body as if it were a bag of feathers. A dark flush stained his face, and he turned to rivet his gaze on Fargo. There was no mistaking the hate.

Fargo didn't plan to speak, but the words just came. "He tried to sneak a shot from that popgun. I suppose you Larrabees set him up."

Luke's mouth was a scar of red and his eyes glowed. "It was his idea, all his, Fargo, to get to you first. We wouldn't set up a thing like that. We wouldn't want you dying that easy."

Fargo quivered with anger. The big ox was seething with hate. "Just keep moving, Luke.

Don't make it easy for me to forget you've got no gun."

Luke nodded. "The first time I saw you, I knew you were a rotten apple. You're a dead man, Fargo; sooner or later we'll get you."

Their eyes locked and Fargo pulled back the hammer of his pistol. "I think I'll make sure you're not around to enjoy it."

It was a frozen moment, but Luke's eyes did not show fear.

"Fargo!" Ruby's voice was on the edge of a scream. She had come down the stairs.

"It's all right, Ruby," Luke said. "Fargo's not much, but he wouldn't shoot an unarmed man."

He kicked the door open and carried out his burden.

Ruby sat down, "Is Luke right? That you wouldn't shoot an unarmed man?"

Fargo thought for a moment, then crunched his teeth. "I've known some human scum in my time, and I'd just as soon shoot them as look at them. But I wouldn't do it to a man like Luke." He jerked his chair more at an angle to the window.

"God, I'll be glad when this day is over," she said. "Poor Matty. The Larrabees must be grieving. They're a tight family, and even if they picked on Matty, he was blood kin. They'll never forgive you, Fargo. If you do get out of Spoon River, they'll hunt you, wherever you go."

"I'll take my chances." He stretched his legs.

"I'm tired," Ruby said. "I'm going to lie down."

It had been a full and fast moving day. But how would it end? he wondered. When the day began, neither Conway nor Matty had any idea they'd be dead. Fargo rubbed his chin. That's the way death hit: when you weren't planning on it.

He thought himself unbeatable, but he could catch a bullet, he knew, easy as most men. He had great speed of draw in a one-on-one, but you didn't always face an even draw. You could be fast, but a lot of guns against you would mow you down. Anything could happen in this territory and in his time he'd seen most things happen. Though he had Ruby as hostage, he had a bad feeling about this setup. He felt boxed in, and he hated that. He was the Trailsman, and he did his best work outdoors, where he knew how to track, how to camouflage. He felt trapped in a house, and had a bad feeling. Using a woman as hostage wasn't his kind of game, either. But survival was the name of the game, and if it took Ruby, then that's the card he'd play.

The die was cast. He'd see it through, no matter how it ended. "María," he called, "bring more coffee."

María, when she came, brought a large mug of coffee. He blew a kiss at María as she went out.

"Fargo." Abigail's voice from down at the boulder.

He watched her move across the lawn, her stride smooth, her figure sexy in the riding pants and boots.

When she came in, her face was serious, and those steady blue eyes studied him. "Fargo, you're in a bad, bad spot."

He didn't feel fear, just a sense of uneasiness. "I've got Ruby."

She saw the bottle. "Can I have some of that?"

He poured her a glass. She sipped it and took a deep breath. She looked a bit pale. She had lived with Matty, after all, and it must have hit her hard, even if she didn't care.

"I'm sorry about Matty," she said. "They told

161

me he acted the fool. Tried to hit you with a hidden gun."

"Not too bright."

She sipped the whiskey. "Always tried to be a big man."

"He made a mistake." Fargo liked looking at Abigail, at those cobalt-blue eyes, that mouth; no matter what she said, the mouth looked saucy.

"Too bad," she said. "I didn't want him dead, though I didn't want to live with him. Not anymore. Not after some of the things he's done." She kept sipping the whiskey. "Where's Ruby?"

"Lying down."

She glanced out the window. "The Larrabees want to eat you alive."

He thought of how they stayed on his trail through the shootings, over the mountain, hanging on like yapping hound dogs. "It would give them a bellyache."

"There's a lot of guns out there, Fargo, and you're holed up in here. Doesn't look good."

"Doesn't look bad either. I've got Ruby." He hitched his belt. "Here's the deal. Tell Terry. They want Ruby, I want to go through. I'm taking her, and if they don't chase, I'll turn her loose in fifteen minutes. But if I go down, she goes, too. Tell them."

Abigail nodded slowly. "Do you trust the Larrabees?"

"Far as I can throw this house. But I've got them. They need Ruby and her dollars. And Terry has big ideas about her future."

"What do you mean?" She looked surprised.

"He's thinking of how to drop Maude and pick up Ruby. I took a lot of trouble one night to find that out."

She looked startled, then her lip curled. "I

thought something smelled, but not that. Terry's a skunk."

They sat silently, and he thought she was one good-looking woman. Her hair glinted in the light from outside.

"Still want me to escort you to Fremont?"

"More than ever, now that Matty's gone."

He frowned. "Why?"

"Terry's always liked the idea of playing games. But he wouldn't cheat his own brother. The Larrabee code. With Matty gone, I expect he'll start trouble."

Larrabee code! Terry was a man without law, who took what he wanted when he wanted it. He dominated the land and felt it gave him domination of women. Now he'd go for Abigail like a coyote for a rabbit.

"Come with me," he said, "when I take Ruby out. After I turn her loose, we'll ride to your home town."

She shook her head. "No good. I'd slow you down."

It was true, the pinto gave him an edge. He'd lose it running with a slower horse. But he wanted to help her.

"I'll take the chance."

"No, it's wrong." She chewed her lip and did some thinking. "If you do get through, we could meet tomorrow, around noon, at the big oak where we met. Remember?"

He grinned. "I remember."

Abigail put down her glass. "I better talk to Ruby."

He called María. "Tell Ruby to come down."

As they waited, Abigail's eyes leveled with his, and the feeling flowing from her made him feel good.

"Take care, Fargo." Her voice was tender.

Ruby came down, and the sight of Abigail made her mouth twist with amusement. "Here she is, the gun girl."

"What do you mean?" Abigail scowled.

"I heard about it. The big deal at the big oak. You pulling your gun on this hot-blooded cowboy." She sneered. "What surprised me is that you didn't want a piece of the cowboy for yourself." She glanced at Fargo with a leer. "Helluva man."

Abigail flushed, turned to Fargo, eyes blazing. "Big talker, aren't you?"

Fargo felt a touch of discomfort. He didn't dream these women would come face to face in a setup like this. He told Ruby the story because it gave him the right to break in, since she was the cause of his trouble. How to explain that to Abigail—he'd let it pass.

Abigail turned to Ruby. "Matty's just dead, and that's all you think of."

"I know how much Matty meant to you," Ruby sneered. "Nothing."

"To be honest, you mean nothing to me," Abigail said coldly. "But we're trying to save your skin. Are you ready to take this deal? Fargo says he'll turn you loose in fifteen minutes if they don't chase."

Ruby shrugged. "Fargo will do what he says."

"Then I'll tell Terry it's all in place."

At the door she turned, and again the cobalt-blue eyes leveled with his. She seemed to have forgiven him for talking about the affair at the big oak.

"Wave when it's all set," he said.

He watched her stride to the boulder. She had her own strength, lots of grit. He studied the terrain—not much cover, once he moved out of the house, but he had Ruby, a guarantee. There was time to make a run for it. He'd go left toward Devil's Crossing. He could drop Ruby as soon as he got out of shooting range, and the pinto would keep him out front. Once on the trail, and minus Ruby, he'd finally get rid of the misery in his bones.

What the hell was happening? They were dragging. Well, they didn't like the idea of letting him through. He wondered what other men Terry had. He stared hard at the boulder; it lay beyond the lawn, down a slope, and gave them strong defense.

Now! A wave from Abigail.

Then a cowboy with a white cloth around his head moved from behind the boulder, holding the reins of two horses, his pinto and a sorrel.

He checked his gun, his eyes swept the landscape. Everything looked right. They'd be insane to try a trick; they wanted Ruby whole, and he'd have a gun on her.

"Let's go," he said to Ruby, and cut the rope binding her wrists. "No funny stuff. I'll turn you loose in a short time." He grimaced. "You can start all over with your precious Terry."

Her expression was strange. "So this is it, Fargo. I'd like to say you're a great hunk of man. Enjoyed having you. But you made a bad mistake coming here. I don't think you'll come out of this alive." Her smile was cool. "But nobody lives forever." She kissed him lightly.

His face was grim. He didn't care for funeral orations. "Go on."

They started to the horses, he standing tight behind her, a bit to the left, his gun clearly visible. There was plenty of light still left. His eye swept the landscape, still clear; they were huddled behind their boulder, under orders not even to peep. The wrangler with the horses, lean and dark-eyed, looked pale, nervous, seemed fearful of what Fargo would do.

Fargo crooked his finger, telling the wrangler to bring the horses closer. He didn't like the position. "Bring the horses back of the house," he said sharply. Better not to give them a target anytime. The one time you were vulnerable to gunfire was when you swung over a saddle. The side of the house gave them protection. They swung over their horses, and he lashed the back of the sorrel as they galloped northwest. Nobody showed, no gun was fired, it went off like clockwork. Almost too good to be true. He smiled. Ruby was the ace card, just as he figured, her moneybags were sacred to the Larrabees.

That was that. He felt a great surge of pleasure to be back on the pinto, out in God's world where he belonged. It made him real sick in the soul to be locked in a house, forced to stay hour after hour. If it ever came to dying, he thought, he wouldn't mind it that much if it just happened out under that great sky, where the great birds spread their wings.

They rode in silence for fifteen minutes, then he grabbed the sorrel's reins and pulled up.

"They must like you an awful lot," he said. "You can go back."

She didn't smile. "I suppose this is the last I'll ever see you alive, Fargo."

"Who knows?" he said, wheeled the pinto, and galloped on.

He rode into high country to kill time and stay clear of pursuit. On the trail he felt power flow back into his body. He found himself thinking of

Abigail. Tomorrow at the big oak, that was the plan. He was glad to help shake her loose from the Larrabees. What kind of a life would she have living close to Terry, low-down and lecherous. Her blond image stuck in his mind that night, sleeping under the big blanket of blue, studded with millions of silver chinks. The sounds of the night—the wail of the lonely coyote, the hoot of the horned owl, the cry of the night hawk—came to him like a background of music.

He slept and the night went on.

Next day, at noon, he approached the great oak with caution. There she was, her back against the tree, in a light blue shirt, a pale silk scarf on her neck, and wearing brown riding britches and boots.

He studied the terrain.

"Were you followed?"

"No, The Larrabees are over at Ruby's. It was easy to come away." She got to her feet. "I can't wait to put distance between us and the Bar-L."

He nodded. "Let's kiss Spoon River good-bye."

12

The horses, it seemed to Fargo, jogged at almost an identical pace as they rode through the countryside. A lush green valley, landscaped beautifully by nature, stretching for miles.

He could see cottonwoods in clusters, a gentle slope, and a stream that, even from this distance, sparkled in the sun. Massive rocks, piled awkwardly on one another here and there, broke out of the earth.

The sun shone gently on all this, and it warmed Fargo's blood. But his blood needed little warming with Abigail riding alongside. She rode a big black, deep-chested and strong-legged, and she rode easy and erect, to give a thrust to her breasts. Her hair shone like spun gold in the sun, and he glanced with enjoyment at her fine, sculptured profile. Of all the women he had known lately, he realized his feeling for her was something special.

He spotted a line cabin at a distance of two miles, a cabin used by cowboys as a shelter on a harsh winter night. Nearby, a small stream flowed, a place to water the horses and wash up.

The sun was still high when they reached it, and he let the horses drink and graze.

The cabin was plain, with a fireplace, a chair, a low wooden bed. He put coffee to boil in the fireplace, brought some hardtack from his saddle-bag. He was thinking he'd shoot some fresh game for dinner, when they moved farther north toward her town.

He looked out the side window at an eagle, its great wings spread, lazily riding the wind. He loved the eagle, a solitary bird, graceful, beautiful, yet a fierce ruler of the skies. The solitary hunter, bird or beast, held a special fascination for him.

"What are you thinking of, Fargo?"

Her eyes on him were curious.

"Just watching the eagle, the way it moves."

She seemed to read his thought. "A loner, something like you. Instead of riding the sky, you ride the land."

He laughed. "I sure did a lot of riding to keep out of the clutches of the Larrabees. It surprised me that they let Ruby and me go through without a trick."

"Surprised me, too," she said. "I thought they'd gun you down."

"There's one thing the Larrabees love more than revenge, and that's money." He studied her. "How would you feel if they did gun me down?"

"Wouldn't like it. No, Fargo, there are some men who should always be alive. Brave, strong men who make life good for others, who make the earth a nicer place to be." She sighed. "There, that should spoil you, Fargo."

He felt his blood sing. "There's one way to spoil me, Abigail."

Her eyes glowed and the power in them made his pulse start to hammer. "What is that?"

He leaned to her, and a tender look came to her face; they gazed into each other's eyes. He put his lips on hers, a tender, soft mouth. He brought her body close to him, kissed her again, and she kissed back passionately. He was astonished at her intensity.

He glanced down; she seemed in a trance of delicious expectation. His hands found her breasts and he caressed them gently. He caressed her body, the slender waist, the curve of her hips. Her breathing came quicker. He reached for the buttons of her shirt, brought out her breasts. They were beautifully shaped, silky-white with delicate pink nipples. He put his lips to them, and her breathing deepened. He brought her down on the bed, pulled at her boots, her pants, her undergarment. She lay nude, her body put together without fault. Her hair spread behind her head like a golden halo, and down between her molded thighs there was a light golden fleece.

She lay waiting as though in some kind of dream. He pulled at his clothes and didn't remember how they came off, but found himself nude beside her, his flesh fiercely alive.

Her eyes seemed to glow with mysterious fire. He felt driven to taste her body with his lips and covered the smooth skin from her breasts to belly down to the tender triangle; he touched her with his tongue, and she quivered as if she'd been stabbed. He played like this for a time, then shifted his body so that she, too, could satisfy her hunger. He felt his flesh enveloped by her mouth, and pleasure flowed through him in great waves. The sight of her passionate concentration sharpened his feelings.

Driven by overpowering impulse, he went over her rounded white body, slipped between her thighs, pierced the silken warmth. He lay, feeling a great rush of sensation; then, goaded by passion, he held her firm buttocks in his palms, began to thrust, his nerves rippling with pleasure.

Her arms were tight about his body, and he felt driven by some great instinctive spirit. The tension in his groin climbed to a pitch, and he hung there and then exploded. A groan escaped from her; she seemed in the grip of some private agony, flung herself against him, held him tight, as if she planned never to let him go.

They stayed for a long time close to each other until the fires cooled, then he pulled away. Her face looked ecstatic, and he couldn't help smiling.

But she said nothing until they were dressed.

After he'd packed and they were ready to saddle up, he said, "The one that got away—she always turns out to be the best."

"Well," she said, her mouth saucy, "you weren't half-bad yourself."

His eyebrows went up. "I was hoping for something better than that."

Amusement glinted in her eyes. "No point spoiling you, Fargo. The Larrabee women have done that. Even Ruby. I don't like to be one of the crowd." She paused.

Then he heard it, the thump, dull, heavy, against the door. His gun came out lightning-fast, and his body, in a crouch, moved low. He jerked the door open, and two feet from his nose lay the body of Ruby, a big red stain on her left breast.

The sight, so far from anything he expected, so jolted him that he froze, unable to put it together in his mind.

"Don't move, Fargo, or you're dead." Terry's voice from the side window.

"Now throw the gun outside the door, throw it far."

Thoughts streaked through his head, a play this way, that way, but it all came to nothing. They had him.

He threw the gun and waited for death.

Nothing.

What were they waiting for? Why didn't they shoot? He remembered Luke's vicious remark: "We wouldn't want you dying that easy."

He looked down at Ruby. A bullet in the heart. Her body in the tight-fitting dress she wore yesterday still looked sexy, with her big breasts and buttocks. All that lust for life gone forever.

He cursed himself. He'd figured wrong about Ruby. They never cared for her, after all, shot her down like a dog. How'd he miss it? She gave them money, she was fixing to become mistress of Bar-L. Was it all phony? He didn't know. But did it matter? He was unarmed and they had guns. They didn't want him dead too fast, wanted a bit of revenge, hard satisfaction. That's the kind of hyenas the Larrabees were.

They came around slowly: Terry with a broad smile; Luke frozen-faced, as usual; two wranglers, men he'd seen at the ranch.

"Come out," Terry said. "The two of you."

When Abigail came out, her face defiant, he looked at her with icy eyes. "Well, little lady, I'm sorry to see you here, consorting with the enemy. The man who shot your husband. That was a very bad thing to do. We'll have to discipline you. Yes, we'll take you home with us later and see if we can't make you see the error of your ways."

Then he turned to Fargo. "Well, you were one tough coyote to hunt down." He studied Fargo's face for fear, and it annoyed him not to see any. "But we got you. We Larrabees get our men, Fargo. You made a stupid mistake when you came to the Bar-L."

Terry looked easy; he had all the cards and could play the game he wanted.

"Why'd you shoot Ruby?" Fargo asked.

Terry's face was all innocence. "Who shot Ruby? Not me. You did, Fargo. You crashed her house, took her as a hostage, and shot her when she tried to escape. That's the story." He turned to the others. "Right, men?"

They all nodded, grinning, except Luke, who watched him like a rattler, waiting for its time to strike.

"I thought you wanted Ruby's moneybags," Fargo said.

Terry looked surprised. "You know an awful lot. I suppose Matty shot his mouth off." He pulled out a cheroot; apparently he was in no hurry, wanted to squeeze the fun out of the setup. "I got most of her money, Fargo. All she's got is a lot of notes. Now what I do is pick them up."

"I thought you cared about her. Wanted to marry her."

Terry scowled. "Now where'd you get that idea? I just joshed her. That slut wanted to become mistress of the Bar-L. Wanted me to dump Maude, a lady I like an awful lot. No, Fargo. Ruby had a lot of dreams. And she had me over a barrel. Then you came along and straightened out everything for me. You're an outlaw. Barged into her home, shot her dead." He stroked his chin. "Mighty kind of you. I owe you a lot, Fargo. Didn't want to mow you down till I could tell you how helpful you were." His gray eyes glittered wickedly.

Fargo took a deep breath. He'd read the whole story wrong and walked into a trap. He realized now why they had blocked him in front of Ruby's. To force him in there. They'd kill two birds with one stone. Get rid of her, blame Fargo. Matty almost spoiled the game, trying to grab Fargo for himself. Matty was always the screw-up.

He glanced at Abigail; she'd been listening from the side, her face a mask, whatever her thoughts, no one could read them.

The men watched him the way you watch a trapped animal. Only Terry held a gun.

"I was thinking," Terry said, "that I might save a bullet if I let Luke give you his compliments."

Luke, as if waiting for this, moved forward, huge of bulk and bone, his broad face in a soft deadly look, the look of a man who, in a gentle manner, would strangle his best friend.

He didn't speak for a full minute, just filling his eyes with the sight of Fargo. "It took a long time to get you," he said finally, "but it's gonna be worth it."

Nobody moved or even breathed at that moment, because of the fearful menace that flowed from his presence. They stood almost toe to toe, eyes locked on each other, and Fargo could read a rage that could be eased only with his death.

"I always meant to ask," Luke said, "if you enjoyed Julia. Did you have a good time at the great oak?"

Fargo shrugged. The Larrabees held him responsible for screwing their women, even if he'd done it at the point of a gun. He should have, he supposed, let himself get shot instead. Rough justice. Well, come to think of it, he really did enjoy Julia, a woman too good for Luke.

The big man, watching, seemed to read his thoughts.

"Fargo, for the next few minutes you just keep in mind the pleasure you got. Because now I'm going to beat you to death with my bare hands."

Terry grinned, and cruelty was all over his face, visualizing the coming slaughter. He turned to Abigail. "You don't have to stay for this."

"I want to," she said.

He scowled at her.

"He killed Matty, didn't he?" she said.

He didn't believe her, but he didn't care as he thought of Matty and all his other grievances.

Terry nodded slowly, his face hard, vicious. "Yeah, he killed Matty, put ten of my men out, raped two Larrabee women. Luke will pay him off."

Luke rolled up his sleeves.

Fargo stared at Luke, a massive head and shoulders, muscular chest, thick, trunklike arms. His one spot of softness, his gut. The trick was to get to that gut before those hamlike fists made contact. A solid hit from Luke would muddle his brains. He was built like a bull, and Fargo, to stay alive, would have to stay fast, light, hit and move.

The broad-boned face was smiling; now, at last, he could unleash the anger and hate that had been seething inside him, since he learned about Julia.

He stepped in and swung a hamlike fist at Fargo; it was ponderous, and Fargo slid under it, moved catlike, threw a hard right at Luke's jaw. Fargo felt the shock through his bone, like hitting rock. The smile slipped from Luke for just a moment, then came back as he swung a right and left, missing. Fargo weaved, danced, and ducked, waiting to lose the numbness in his arm. No point hitting that massive face, it was all stone. The gut, the gut. He swung hard and low. Luke flinched. The gut, he swung again and connected.

Luke roared, swung a roundhouse, then stomped

forward. Fargo backed up, lost his balance, fell. Luke rushed, brought his giant boot to kick; Fargo twisted away, caught part of the kick, felt the scrape and the bruise. The iron boot went up to kick again. Fargo grabbed it and twisted with all his might. Luke lost his balance and fell. Fargo fought the urge to kick his skull. Luke'd have done it. His face twisted in a rage, Luke scrambled to his feet, and with unexpected speed, rushed, managed to grab Fargo's arm and pull him into a crushing bear embrace.

Fargo felt his breath squeezed from his lungs and, as the vise tightened, his back beginning to crack. Another moment and his back would break. He brought the heel of his hand up, like a mule's kick, under Luke's nose, felt the tear of the nostrils. The shock made Luke loosen his grip, and Fargo brought his knee hard into the soft gut; heard the hoarse grunt as he slipped out of the killing embrace. Luke put a hand to his nose, looked at the streaming blood, and his eyes glazed with maniacal rage. He rushed wildly.

Fargo stepped aside, drove his fist hard, with shoulder behind it, again into the soft gut. Luke looked green as Fargo hit again, feeling the soft flesh give way. Luke's wild backhand caught Fargo on the side of the head, spun him; the shock flashed through his body, and his nerves went numb. He stood dazed. As Luke scrambled toward him, Fargo tried to back off; but Luke swung again, hit his cheek, and Fargo's head snapped back and his brain went dark for a moment. If he didn't escape the reach of those fists, he'd be pounded to death in minutes.

Luke kept coming. Fargo backed away, moving right, left, fighting for time as the fog cleared. Then Luke grabbed his left arm and was swing-

ing him in for his death hug, to break his spine.
He had to do something or he was a dead man.
Luke's head was high, his face in a fiendish grin
of expectation, his gaze up, as if thanking heaven,
his throat was open. As he swung in, Fargo drove
his iron fist like a piston at Luke's Adam's apple,
felt the crunch of bone as it pushed into the
throat. A frozen moment, then the massive hands
left him as Luke grabbed for his throat, trying to
patch it together, making raucous, hoarse noises
as he fought for breath. His face turned red, he
made horrible inhaling sounds, his eyes seemed
to squeeze from their sockets as he stared at
Fargo. Then he dropped with a thump to the
earth, his hands still at his throat, squirming and
strangling. Slowly his body stopped heaving and
his skin started to turn blue. He lay silent, a
huge bulk, suffocated by his own crushed throat.

The men had watched with horror, helpless.

Racked, bruised, and exhausted, Fargo shifted
his sight from Luke to Terry. The gray eyes were
glazed with horror as he watched the death throes
of his brother. Then he tore his gaze from the
slumped figure to Fargo, slowly raising his gun.
Fargo saw his death in those eyes.

Terry's mouth opened, but the words at first
didn't come. Then he found his voice.

"If only there was a hundred ways to kill you.
But I'm going to shoot you to pieces. Going to
shoot your balls off first, then pick at the rest of
you. Just shoot you to pieces and let you die
slow. Plenty of time to think about what you did
to the Larrabees."

He lowered the gun, aiming carefully at Fargo's
groin. Fargo waited for the bullet. The shot rang
out, but he didn't feel it. The sadistic bastard
deliberately missed.

Terry had turned to look with a strange expression at Abigail. She had Fargo's gun and she was watching Terry. Fargo looked again at Terry, then saw the blood pumping from his chest. He fell to his knees, still looking at Abigail in amazement. Then he turned to Fargo and struggled to raise his gun. He tried with a giant effort, the sweat in big drops coming out on his forehead. The gun went higher and higher. Everyone watched, hypnotized; then Terry squeezed the trigger, but the bullet went wild. The gun trembled in his hand, and he stared at Fargo, his eyes with an unholy glow, his mouth wrenched with hate. He seemed to be fighting death because he was going unrevenged. Then his eyes went empty, and he fell facedown on the earth. He didn't even twitch.

Everyone had watched his death throes as if in a trance.

Abigail swung her gun on the wranglers, but they wanted no part of anything now.

"The guns," said Fargo, "drop 'em and git!"

They dropped their guns, hustled hard to their horses behind the boulders, and rode off fast.

Fargo gazed at Abigail. He grinned.

Then he shut his eyes and collapsed on the floor.

It was almost sundown, and as they cantered along, he couldn't help taking another look at her with a tinge of regret. If ever a woman appealed more to him, he didn't know how.

She looked at him with those beautiful blue eyes and sighed. "I know you're not a man to put down roots. It'd be bad for me to lose my head over a man who'd just break my heart. You're always going off somewheres, aren't you, Fargo?"

178

His face clouded. "I have to go."

"Why?"

His eyes were stony. "I can't stop now. I've got to keep searching for two men who've got to pay for what they did to my family. Until it's finished, I can't put down roots."

She smiled sadly. "So you're the lover who got away."

"But I may come back," he said.

The sun glowed in the sky as they rode along the trail.

LOOKING FORWARD

The following is the opening section
from the next novel in the exciting new
Trailsman series from Signet:

THE TRAILSMAN #20:
THE JUDAS KILLER

*Nevada, 1861, when the gambling
was whether a man could stay alive.
The southern foothills of
the Ruby Mountains . . .*

"Dammit, Dixie, you promised me peace, quiet, and a good roll in the hay, nothing else," Fargo protested.

"You been getting that. Hell, we hardly been out of that bed for two days," the woman answered.

Fargo watched her as she stood naked beside the cabin window, peering out, concern digging a frown into her forehead. Dixie Treadwell had always been an ample woman, he recalled; even as a young girl ten years ago she was slightly heavy. Broad features, surrounded by brown hair, a face more arresting than pretty. Large, over-flowing breasts with big, pink-brown nipples, a rounded belly, rear a little heavy, and full-fleshed thighs, but all of a piece, all fitting together with an earthy sex, an easy-riding woman.

"Fargo, you can't just lay there and let this go on. Come look for yourself," Dixie called, her gaze staying focused out the window.

Fargo heaved a deep sigh from the bottom of his chest and swung long legs and a hard-muscled frame from the bed. Dixie had risen when she'd heard the distant shouts and had stayed glued to the window.

"Hell, that's just a little boy out there," she said, as Fargo started toward her. "He can't be more than twelve and those three big galoots are trying to run him down."

Fargo halted at her side, leaned against the smooth fullness of her body, and followed her gaze to the slope of a foothill just above the ridge that hid the little cabin from prying eyes. She was right about the boy, he saw; the youngster was most likely not past twelve. The boy rode a dark-brown quarterhorse and tried desperately to elude the three men who were trying to hem him in. He was doing a pretty good job of it, Fargo noted, as he wheeled his quarterhorse in tight, darting patterns. But he was tiring, Fargo saw, the three men coming closer with each attempt at rushing him.

"You get out there and see what that's all about, Fargo," Dixie demanded. "I don't like the look of it."

As he watched, Fargo saw the boy make a wrong turn and one of his pursuers move in fast. Panicked, the boy made another mistake, tried to send his horse in a straight spurt between the other two men. But the horse didn't have enough speed left in him and the two men had the angle in their favor. Fargo saw them converging on the boy and he turned from the window. "All right, you win," he muttered to Dixie. "I'll get dressed and have a look."

"They've got him," he heard Dixie cry out. "They've knocked him off his horse. Christ, they're kicking him." Fargo started to reach for his pants, halted at Dixie's scream. "There's no time to dress. Just get out there before they kill that kid."

"Shit," Fargo muttered as he grabbed his gun belt and strapped it on as he ran from the cabin. Clad only in the belt with the big Colt .45 in the holster, he vaulted onto the unsaddled Ovaro outside and sent the horse into a gallop. He felt the smooth warmth of the horse through his thighs and buttocks, the oneness of horse and rider the red man knew so well. The path to the slope led down and around the base of the foothill, far too long a way, he decided, and sent the pinto up a steep incline few horses could negotiate, and toward a ridge that would bring him directly onto the condalia-covered slope.

Damn Dixie, he swore silently, she had always been one for going to the aid of any stray, four-footed or two-footed. Until he rode into Jimson two days ago, he hadn't seen Dixie in five years. But the time vanished quickly, so quickly that she had pulled back. "I've a good reputation here in Jimson," she'd said. "The head of the women's church bazaar commitee can't go shacking up with some stranger that rides into town."

"Not even an old friend?" he had said.

"Not even. Nobody here knows about the old days of Dixie Treadwell, and I intend to keep it that way," she'd answered.

"You want me to keep riding?" he had asked.

"You know I don't," Dixie had snapped. "I've

done too much remembering over the years to let you just ride on." She'd told him about the cabin then, her own little hideaway, and he'd gone to it, was waiting there when she arrived.

The boy's sharp cry of pain broke into his thoughts as he topped the ridge. The three men had dismounted, one holding the boy on the ground and slapping his head back and forth while the other two watched. All three turned as Fargo rode across the slope. He saw the astonishment in their eyes and couldn't begrudge them that much.

"Jesus, I thought I'd seen everything," one said from under a dirty-gray Stetson. The man holding the boy stared at the all-but-naked rider out of little button eyes and kept his knee on the boy's chest.

"Let the boy up," Fargo said, reining to a halt.

"Who the hell are you, some kind of freak?" the one with the dirty-gray hat asked. The third man just watched, his lined face grim.

Fargo's lips were a thin line and he silently swore at Dixie. It was more than a little hard to be impressive in his naked attire.

"Let the boy up," he repeated.

The man grinned from under the Stetson. "I know, you wanted to prove you've got balls? Okay, we've seen 'em. Now get the hell out of here, freak," he said. He was too busy grinning to see the blue-ice in the naked man's eyes.

"I don't need clothes on to shoot," Fargo said softly.

The man's grin vanished, became a half-snarl. "Fuck off or I'll put a bullet up your bare ass," he said.

"Kill him," the one holding the boy growled.

Fargo saw the man with the Stetson immediately go for his gun. He never got it out of its holster as the big black-haired man's Colt seemed to leap from its holster with a will of its own. The gun barked once and the man's head seemed to all but fly from his shoulders as he half-somersaulted backwards, and suddenly the dirty-gray became a dull red. The second man managed to get his gun out from his holster, but the big Colt moved a fraction of an inch to the left and barked again. The man went backwards with a kind of strange shuffle before sinking to the ground to lay in a twisted heap.

Fargo saw the third man dive forward into a row of thick condalia shrub, taking the boy with him. There was no chance for a clean shot and Fargo executed a backward half-flip from the pinto, anticipating the two shots that came a split second later. Fargo rolled into a thicket of the condalia, came up on his stomach, the Colt ready to fire. He saw the brush move a half-dozen yards away, but the man stayed out of sight with the boy. Fargo moved, winced. The rough thicket had jabbed him in the groin. Less than a half-minute passed before he heard the man's voice.

"You out there, throw your gun out," the man called.

Fargo stayed silent.

"The gun, throw it out, or the kid gets it. I'll blast his damn head off," the man called again.

"No, you won't," Fargo called back.

"The hell I won't," he heard the man shout.

"He's your ace card only while he's alive. You shoot him and you're a dead man, guaranteed," Fargo returned. "You keep him alive and you stay alive." Fargo listened to the silence and

knew the man cursed in angry frustration, all too
aware the strange naked man had called his bluff
correctly. "Let the boy go and you can ride away
alive," he called.

"Just like that, eh?" the man returned.

"You've my word on it," Fargo said.

"Maybe that don't mean shit," the man replied.

Fargo nodded to himself. He could understand
the man's answer. He'd probably give the same,
if positions were reversed. He thought for a
moment, lifted his voice again. "You can take the
boy in the saddle with you, ride a hundred yards.
That's plenty far out of six-gun range. Let the
boy go there and keep riding," Fargo said.

He waited, let the man turn over the offer.
"What if I keep riding with him?" the man asked.

"You won't make another hundred yards, I
promise you," Fargo said.

Another moment of silence and then the man's
voice called again, a new respect in it. "Who the
hell are you, mister?" he asked.

"Fargo ... Skye Fargo. Some call me the
Trailsman," the big black-haired man answered.

"All right, I'm comin' out. Anything tricky and
I'll blast the kid," the man called. Fargo stayed
behind the shrub as he saw the man rise, a gun
held to the boy's bloodied cheek. The man moved
from the condalia with the boy held in front of
him, backed toward his horse. He was perspiring,
Fargo saw, his forehead shining, his little eyes
blinking nervously.

Fargo remained out of sight as the man mounted
his horse from the other side, kept the gun against
the boy's face. He pulled the boy up with him,
kept one thick arm around the boy's waist, using
the slender figure as a shield. He sent the horse

into a fast canter, and Fargo rose from the shrub and stepped to the Ovaro. He pulled himself onto the horse, his lake-blue eyes narrowed, held unwaveringly on the rider moving away. Fargo counted off yards, started to push his knees into the pinto's ribs when he saw the man halt and the small figure slip to the ground. Fargo sent the pinto forward as the man raced his horse away at a full gallop.

The boy was still standing when Fargo reached him, his young face bloodied and bruised. Fargo swung from the pinto, put a hand on the boy's shoulder. "You're safe now, son," he said, put his hand on the boy's shoulder, and felt the small figure tremble.

"Thanks to you, mister," the boy said, and Fargo saw his eyes flick over his nakedness.

"I usually wear more than this," Fargo said. He lifted the boy onto the pinto, swung on behind him, and turned the horse around. "Can you ride on your own?" he asked when he reached the boy's quarterhorse.

The boy nodded, climbed onto his horse as Fargo drew the pinto up alongside it. Fargo saw the boy eye him again from under swollen brows. The boy had been knocked around plenty, but he was still sharp, hurt but unshaken. There was a toughness in that slender frame, Fargo decided.

"You said your name was Fargo?" the boy questioned, and Fargo nodded. "Never saw anyone shoot that fast, Mr. Fargo," the boy said. "With or without clothes," he added.

"Follow me," Fargo said, turned the pinto down the long way. It was easier riding, and when he reached the little cabin, he saw Dixie, in skirt and blouse, rush out to meet them. Her round face wreathed in horror as she saw the boy's bloodied and battered face.

"You just come with me," she said, helping him from the horse. "You must hurt all over."

"I'm all right," the boy said as Fargo saw him wince with pain. No fake bravery, he decided. Tough little customer, he concluded again as Dixie led the boy into the cabin.

Fargo took the quarterhorse to the side of the cabin and tethered the animal, let the Ovaro graze on his own. When he returned to the cabin, Dixie had washed the caked blood from the boy's face, had him lying on the bed with his shirt off. He seemed smaller, more the little boy with slender arms and a boy's unmuscled body. But the strength was there in the set of his little chin, a certain stoic quality in his dark-brown eyes set in a square face topped with short brown hair. Dixie was applying salve from a small crock to the boy's bruises.

"Powder made from the bark of the slippery elm mixed with lobelia," she said. "It'll take the pain out of those bruises in no time."

"Thank you, ma'am," the boy murmured.

"Call me Dixie," Fargo heard Dixie say. He pulled on shorts and trousers, then the rest of his clothes, and felt less foolish-looking. He leaned against the wall and the boy met his gaze.

"You want to tell us what this is all about?" he said. "Start with your name."

"Bobby," the boy said. "Bobby Darrow."

"Who were those men, Bobby?" Fargo asked.

"I don't know," Bobby Darrow said. "They just started chasing me."

"For no reason?" Fargo questioned.

"Oh, they had a reason. They wanted the medicine," Bobby Darrow said.

"The medicine?" Fargo echoed.

"Yes, sir." Bobby nodded, his little face grave.

"You know what the men wanted, but you don't know who they were," Fargo said, and the boy nodded. "This isn't making a hell of a lot of sense, Bobby. Suppose we start over. What medicine?"

"The medicine for the wagon train," Bobby said.

Dixie had stopped rubbing the salve on him. "What wagon train, Bobby?" she cut in.

"The one up in the Ruby Mountains," the boy said.

"You came from a wagon train?" Dixie pressed.

"Yes, ma'am. I came to get the medicine and bring it back to them," Bobby answered.

"They sent you, a little boy?" Dixie frowned.

Bobby nodded gravely. "I was the only one who could go. Half the wagon train is real sick. There's some that have died. It was decided that the few men still well had to stay there. That's Shoshoni country up there. We've seen signs."

"Paiute and Nez Percé, too. Sometimes the Chiricahua Apache get up that far," Fargo said.

"What are they sick with, Bobby? Not the plague or smallpox?" Dixie asked anxiously.

"No, but there's a real bad fever, the killing kind, and chills and aching," Bobby said. "Doc Anderson, he's with the train, he was taking care of it pretty well until he ran out of medicine. Then folks started dying. The doc said it'd get worse unless he got some more medicine. He said there was a doctor in Jimson who used the kind of medicine he needed."

"In Jimson? That'd be Doc Bellows," Dixie said.

"Yes, ma'am, that's where I went," Bobby said.

"I still can't see sending a young boy." Dixie frowned again.

"There was nobody else, Miss Dixie. Besides, I was the lightest. I could make the best time on a good horse, and Doc said every minute counted. He gave me directions to Jimson and I went," Bobby said. "Only got lost twice," he added with a touch of pride.

"Tell me about those three men again," Fargo asked.

"Last night, after I left the doc's with the medicine, they came at me," Bobby said. "I got away from them in the dark and hid the medicine. I waited till morning and started out again. I thought they'd leave me alone when they saw I didn't have the medicine."

Fargo nodded. Bobby could think on his feet. He was shrewd as well as tough. "They say why they wanted the medicine?" he queried.

"No, sir. They just said they wanted it," Bobby answered.

"That medicine, did Doc Bellows tell you whether he had any more?" Dixie interjected.

"That was the last of it. He said it'd be a month before he got any more," Bobby said.

"There's your answer," Dixie said to Fargo. "They need it for somebody or someplace, found out that Bobby had the last of it, and went after him for it."

"Maybe," Fargo muttered.

"Maybe?" Dixie questioned.

"Kind of a strange coincidence, their needing

the same medicine at the same time," Fargo commented.

Dixie was digesting his words when Bobby's voice cut in. "Thank you both very much," the boy said, "but I've got to be moving on."

"Moving on?" Dixie frowned in protest as Bobby pulled on his shirt. "You're in no condition to go on."

"I don't feel too good, but I've got to go," Bobby said to her, his eyes wide. "I've lost enough time. I've got to get that medicine back to the wagons before it's too late."

"You think you can find your way back?" Dixie asked.

Fargo saw Bobby shrug, look suddenly uncertain. "I don't know. I have to try," he said, and Fargo saw Dixie's concern spiraling.

"And what about those men? One got away. He could be watching for you, maybe with others," Dixie said.

Bobby shrugged and tossed Dixie a glance of helpless bravery. "I'll have to chance it, Miss Dixie," he said.

Fargo's eyes narrowed. The kid was playing Dixie's built-in concern for all it was worth. Why? Fargo started to wonder. Then Bobby's next words supplied one reason.

"I wish I didn't have to go alone, but I can't do anything about that," he heard Bobby say, once more with touching bravery.

The little con man, Fargo muttered silently, and watched Dixie take the bait the way a trout takes a minnow.

"I can do something about it, Bobby," she said.

"Could you really, Miss Dixie?" Bobby said with just the right touch of grateful hope.

Excerpt from THE JUDAS KILLER

The little bastard, Fargo growled to himself. He was playing it to the hilt. Fargo saw Dixie turn to him and he knew exactly she was going to say.

And exactly what he was going to answer.